*She'd longed for his touch
from the day she'd met him.*

Now it was gentle as his thumb brushed her cheekbone. But when he ruffled the hair at her temple, he suddenly stilled.

"That's a scar," he said, tracing his finger over it. "What happened?"

She could tell him why she'd come to him, why she'd sought him out, but she knew her feelings for him were growing deeper. She didn't want him to send her away. He'd do that if she told him about the dreams. He'd think she was crazy.

"I was in an accident. It's still too painful to talk about."

After he studied her for a moment, he said, "I don't like talking about the past, either." His hand moved from her face to the nape of her neck. He murmured, "Maybe we can forget about it altogether." And then his lips came down on hers.

* * *

Don't miss next month's SOULMATES title— *Cassie's Cowboy,* by Diane Pershing!

Dear Reader,

Calling all royal watchers! This month, Silhouette Romance's Carolyn Zane kicks off our exciting new series, ROYALLY WED: THE MISSING HEIR, with the gem *Of Royal Blood.* Fans of last year's ROYALLY WED series will love this thrilling four-book adventure, filled with twists and turns—and of course, plenty of love and romance. Blue bloods and commoners alike will also enjoy Laurey Bright's newest addition to her VIRGIN BRIDES thematic series, *The Heiress Bride,* about a woman who agrees to marry to protect the empire that is rightfully hers.

This month is also filled with earth-shattering secrets! First, award-winning author Sharon De Vita serves up a whopper in her latest SADDLE FALLS title, *Anything for Her Family.* Natalie McMahon is much more than the twin boys' nanny— she's their mother! And in Karen Rose Smith's *A Husband in Her Eyes,* the heroine has her eyesight restored, only to have haunting visions of a man and child. Can she bring love and happiness back into their lives?

Everyone likes surprises, right? Well, in Susan Meier's *Married Right Away,* the heroine certainly gives her boss the shock of his life—she's having his baby! And Love Inspired author Cynthia Rutledge makes her Silhouette Romance debut with her modern-day Cinderella story, *Trish's Not-So-Little Secret,* about "Fatty Patty" who comes back to her hometown a beautiful swan—and a single mom with a jaw-dropping secret!

We hope this month that you feel like a princess and enjoy the royal treats we have for you from Silhouette Romance.

Happy reading!

Mary-Theresa Hussey

Mary-Theresa Hussey
Senior Editor

Please address questions and book requests to:
Silhouette Reader Service
U.S.: 3010 Walden Ave., P.O. Box 1325, Buffalo, NY 14269
Canadian: P.O. Box 609, Fort Erie, Ont. L2A 5X3

A Husband in Her Eyes

KAREN ROSE SMITH

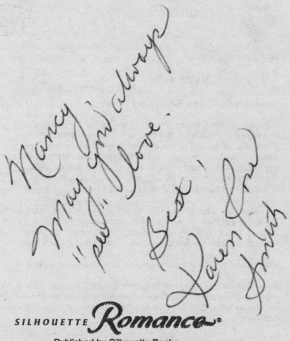

Nancy,
May God's always
"purr" love.
Best,
Karen Rose
Smith

SILHOUETTE *Romance*®

Published by Silhouette Books

America's Publisher of Contemporary Romance

With deepest appreciation
to Marlene and Ken Urso—my California consultants—
as well as to firefighter Dominick Kass,
who always gives me thorough answers to my questions.

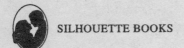 SILHOUETTE BOOKS

ISBN 0-373-19577-X

A HUSBAND IN HER EYES

Copyright © 2002 by Karen Rose Smith

This edition published by arrangement with Harlequin Books S.A.

Visit Silhouette at www.eHarlequin.com

Printed in U.S.A.

Books by Karen Rose Smith

Silhouette Romance

*Adam's Vow #1075
*Always Daddy #1102
*Shane's Bride #1128
†Cowboy at the Wedding #1171
†Most Eligible Dad #1174
†A Groom and a Promise #1181
The Dad Who Saved
  Christmas #1267
‡Wealth, Power and a
  Proper Wife #1320
‡ Love, Honor and a
  Pregnant Bride #1326
‡Promises, Pumpkins and
  Prince Charming #1332
The Night Before Baby #1348
‡Wishes, Waltzes and a Storybook
  Wedding #1407
Just the Man She Needed #1434
Just the Husband She Chose #1455
Her Honor-Bound Lawman #1480
Be My Bride? #1492
Tall, Dark & True #1506
Her Tycoon Boss #1523
Doctor in Demand #1536
A Husband in Her Eyes #1577

Silhouette Special Edition

Abigail and Mistletoe #930
The Sheriff's Proposal #1074
His Little Girl's Laughter #1426

Silhouette Books

The Fortunes of Texas
Marry in Haste...

*Darling Daddies
†The Best Men
‡ Do You Take This Stranger?

Previously published under the pseudonym Kari Sutherland

Silhouette Romance

Heartfire, Homefire #973

Silhouette Special Edition

Wish on the Moon #741

KAREN ROSE SMITH

is a former teacher and home decorator. Now spinning stories and creating characters keeps her busy. But she also loves listening to music, shopping and sharing with friends, as well as spending time with her son and her husband. Married for thirty years, she and her husband have always called Pennsylvania home. Karen Rose likes to hear from readers. They can write to her at P.O. Box 1545, Hanover, PA 17331 or visit her Web site at www.karenrosesmith.com.

Dear Reader,

I'm so pleased to have the opportunity to write
A Husband in Her Eyes. I've been nurturing this idea
since the eighties when I saw a talk show concerning
transplant donors and recipients. When I researched
corneal transplants then, medical technology wasn't
advanced enough to lend realism to the book. But last
year when my editor invited me to write an innovative
project, I researched my concept again and found that
medical advances now made my idea feasible. Mingling
the scientific with the spiritual and emotional was an
exciting process.

I believe in mystery and miracles, as well as not
always being able to discover the answers to the
time-honored questions. I also believe the power of
love is the strongest force in the universe and makes
the impossible possible. Love draws my heroine into my
hero's life. Having the courage to unravel the mystery of
her dreams leads her to her soulmate. There is no greater
joy than fulfilling destiny by seeking and finding lifelong
love.

As you read Zack and Melanie's love story, I hope you
will believe along with me.

All my best,

Karen Rose Smith

Prologue

He was tall, with dark brown hair...and deep, deep brown eyes that were anguished and so very sad. He was standing in the rain, gazing up at the mountains and calling to someone. A pair of pink-and-blue baby booties dangled from the peak of the mountain.

Melanie Carlotti awakened. Her eyes flew open, and she sat up and hugged her pillow. This man who haunted her dreams caused such a yearning inside of her. Heart pounding and breathless, she ran her fingers through her short, light brown hair and glanced at the clock in her bedroom. It was 3:00 a.m. She knew she wouldn't be going back to sleep tonight. How many nights had she spent wandering the apartment after a dream of the handsome stranger?

Switching on her bedside lamp, she wished the dreams would stop. But then as she slid her legs over the side of the bed, she knew that wasn't altogether true. Ever since her corneal transplants, these images had flitted through her mind and her dreams. The man's face was clear to her, and she didn't understand the yearning of her heart to reach out to him.

Restlessly she crossed to her rolltop desk and picked up the framed photograph of the husband and little girl she'd lost, lovingly tracing her finger around Kaitlyn's four-year-old face. Tears came to Melanie's eyes as she stared at her husband. She'd particularly reminded Phil to unplug the Christmas tree lights before he went to bed that night....

It wasn't Phil's face she saw in her dreams...and the feelings that overwhelmed her now didn't seem to belong to her. She couldn't go on like this.

For the past few months she'd tried to find the identity of her organ donor. The problem was, the identity of donors as well as recipients was kept strictly confidential. She *had* to find out what these dreams meant. She had to find out who her organ donor was, and if the dreams and her operation were truly connected.

Rolling up the lid on the desk, she pushed aside the contract and pictures from her most recent interior decorating job, took out the phone book and flipped to the yellow pages. A few moments later she found the section she was looking for—private investigators.

Somehow she was going to make sense of all of this. Somehow she'd find the identity of the man in her dreams. Then she could go on with her life.

Chapter One

The woman who opened the penthouse door was only five feet tall, with snow-white hair and twinkling green eyes. She wore sensible brown-and-white tie shoes, denim overalls and a plaid blouse. "Melanie Carlotti?" she asked, confirming Melanie's appointment.

"Yes. I know I'm a little early, but since I wasn't exactly sure where I was going—"

"We're in the middle of nowhere," the woman agreed with a grin. "But not for long, I imagine." She gave Melanie a quick once-over. "I'm Flo Briggs, Mr. Morgan's housekeeper. Follow me and I'll take you to his office."

Melanie took a deep breath, nervous about this appointment. Not only about the appointment. She felt as if she were being led by an unseen hand, and the idea gave her a shivery feeling. Through her private investigator's competent search of medical records and death certificates, she'd found out her corneal transplant donor had been Sherry Morgan from Santa Rosa. Her husband, Zachary Morgan, was a self-made businessman who owned a chain of sports equipment stores.

And he was looking for an interior decorator to put the finishing touches on his new office building an hour north of Santa Rosa.

Simply a coincidence?

The P.I. had offered to get her a picture of Zachary Morgan. But Melanie had needed to find out more about Sherry Morgan's life…to meet her husband in person and figure out exactly what the feelings she was experiencing were all about.

In just a few moments she'd find out whether he *was* the man in her dreams. If he was…

Melanie's heart thudded so hard, she felt as if it were going to jump out of her chest as Flo Briggs led her past a spacious living room, then down a hall. There the housekeeper motioned to an open door.

Melanie stepped inside and came face-to-face with Zachary Morgan. Her organ donor's husband was sitting at his desk, his white, oxford-cloth shirtsleeves rolled up, deeply involved in his work and seemingly oblivious to her presence.

This is the man, everything inside of her screamed. She felt almost dizzy with the realization that her dreams had been much more than dreams.

As he stood to greet her, their eyes locked and Melanie's heart lurched.

"Miss Carlotti?" he asked, his voice deep and rich, striking a chord inside of her. He extended his hand, and for a moment she was afraid to take it.

Then she did. His grip was strong, his skin warm, his hand tanned, and she was so relieved when she didn't feel anything strange. "Yes. It's good to meet you."

Releasing her fingers, he leaned away and nodded to the black leather chair in front of his desk. "Tell me why you'd like to decorate my offices."

After she took her seat, he lowered himself into his chair but kept his gaze on hers. She still couldn't believe she was finally in the presence of the man she'd been dreaming about for months—a man she'd found so very compelling. Yet she knew if she told him her real reason for being here, he wouldn't believe her or worse yet, he'd think she was crazy.

Smoothing her hand down the rose skirt of her two-piece dress, she gave a logical explanation for wanting this job. "The way I understand it, this is a large project—four floors of offices. I'd enjoy working on a job that size, starting from scratch and choosing everything from wall coverings to furniture."

He glanced down briefly at the papers on his desk. "You've mostly decorated homes. Why do you feel you have the qualifications to do this job?"

"I'd expect you'd want your offices to reflect something about you and your business and how you run it. It's really not so different from decorating a house to match a client's personality as well as likes and dislikes."

"I suppose that's so." Keeping his gaze steady on hers, he said, "There's almost a two-year gap in your work history, and you've only finished a couple of minor jobs in the past few months. Can you tell me the reason for that?"

She could lay it all out on his desk right now—tell him about the fire and her corneal transplants and the keening ache that had brought her to him. If she did that, he might escort her out of his building, lock the doors and never let her back in. She'd be left with dreams and no explanations. "I had some health problems," she explained. "Now they're resolved and I'm ready to get back into the swing of my career again."

He seemed to think about that. "Why here in Northern California rather than back in L.A.?"

"I need a change. I've heard that Santa Rosa is a particularly lovely place to live. I have a good reputation that I can take with me anywhere, so I decided to start fresh. *If* I get this job."

He arched a brow. "And if you don't?"

"I might stay for a while and see if there are any other opportunities."

After another long, silent appraisal, he asked, "Do you have a place to stay?"

"Not yet. I checked into the motel at Cool Ridge last night." Cool Ridge was about forty-five minutes outside of Santa Rosa and consisted of little more than a main street. She'd been fortunate to find a room in the one motel there. A country-music festival was being held at nearby Clear Lake, and vacancies were hard to find anywhere in the area.

As her gaze held Zachary Morgan's, there seemed to be more than words between them. Something akin to electricity. She wondered if he felt it, too.

His brows furrowed as he once again looked down at the papers on his desk, and she suspected he was buying time as he made a first impression of her. "Your résumé is certainly complete. I phoned—".

Suddenly a toddler came running into the office. From her P.I.'s report, Melanie knew Zack's daughter was eighteen months old. The little girl made a beeline straight for Zack and held on to his knee, looking up at him with a beatific smile.

Melanie's breath caught at the wave of feelings that

washed over her. Zack's daughter had dark brown eyes and his dark brown hair, but where his was thick with a slight wave, the child's was fine and fell in ringlets framing her face.

"Da-dee. Up," she said gleefully.

Flo Briggs came tearing into the office, breathless. "I'm so sorry, Zack. She got away from me. Right after her nap, she's got more energy than ten of me."

Zack laughed and lifted his daughter onto his lap. "How's a man supposed to conduct business with a distraction like you around?" His voice was teasing and warm and altogether loving.

"Da-dee, Da-dee," she said, as if that explained absolutely everything.

He shook his head. "I can't play right now. Maybe Flo can find a cookie or two for you."

As if telling her dad that was a fine idea, the child wrapped her arms around his neck and gave him a tight squeeze.

He hugged her back and, looking over her tiny shoulder, he said to Melanie, "This is my daughter, Amy. Since we moved here I often work out of the penthouse, and she takes advantage of any time she can find me."

Amy suddenly let go of her dad's neck and turned to look at Melanie.

Melanie had felt an almost hum when her gaze had first connected with Zachary Morgan's. Now as she looked at his daughter, there was that same feeling of connection. Was it her imagination? Truth be told, if she hadn't already been dealing with strange things since her operation, she might think she *was* going crazy.

Her heart told her another story…especially when Amy blinked twice at her, broke into a superwide smile and scrambled from her dad's lap. She ran to Melanie and looked up at her with wide brown eyes.

"Hi, there," Melanie said almost reverently, feeling like a mother again. Joy and sadness and an unfathomable yearning filled her.

Amy held her arms up, never taking her gaze from Melanie's. Instinctively she lifted the toddler to her lap. The little girl touched Melanie's cheek, her soft baby fingers leaving an imprint on Melanie's heart.

Flo Briggs rushed over, a surprised expression on her face. "She *never* goes to strangers," Flo murmured. Then she looked at Melanie's pretty rose dress and Amy's little shoes. "C'mon, poppet. We don't want to get Ms. Carlotti all dirty." The housekeeper gathered up the little girl into her arms. Flo assured her employer with a wink, "We'll find a cookie and some juice and play with blocks for a while. Then maybe you can get some work done."

When Melanie glanced at Zack, he was staring at her as if he were searching for the reason Amy had taken to her. Then he stood and came around the desk, kissed Amy's forehead and ruffled her hair.

Amy waved at Melanie as Flo carried her out of the room.

In front of his desk now, Zack Morgan was only two feet away from Melanie, and she could smell the forest scent of his cologne. Given his at-least-six-foot height and his very broad shoulders, he seemed to take up the entire office. Maybe it was just her awareness of him that took up the entire office.

As he leaned against his desk, his gaze was inscrutable. "Your résumé doesn't say whether or not you're married."

Amy's touch still tingled on Melanie's cheek. "I was

once. I'm not married now." She couldn't tell him more than that without revealing too much.

"Is that the reason you left L.A.?"

"One of them," she answered quietly. There was a straightforwardness in Zack Morgan's attitude that urged her to tell him everything. But she couldn't. Not yet.

Silence lingered between them for a few moments. Finally Zack broke it. "Let's go take a look at the offices. When we're finished, you can give me ideas. If I like them, we'll talk about a contract."

When Melanie stood, she found herself very close to Zack. "Now?"

"Yes. Unless there's somewhere else you have to be this afternoon."

His brown eyes were almost challenging, and she suspected anyone who worked with Zack Morgan needed a backbone. "No. I don't have any other appointments today. I planned to give your project my full attention."

He nodded. "Okay. Let's see what your attention can do for my new workspace."

As they left the penthouse, Melanie could hear Zack's daughter jabbering and giggling in the kitchen. She remembered her own daughter's laughter…her first word…her first tooth…her first step. The memories were less painful now and more bittersweet, yet she knew the missing would never go away, and she hoped the memories would never fade. They were too precious.

Zack's legs were long, and he covered the distance to the elevator a lot sooner than Melanie did. She suspected he was a man who always knew where he was going and how he wanted to get there.

As they stepped onto the elevator, his elbow brushed hers and her throat went dry. She couldn't ever remember feeling this affected by a man. Not even by her husband.

The elevator door swished shut.

Zack tried to keep his gaze straight ahead instead of on Melanie as he collected his thoughts and analyzed his reaction to this woman. There was such a pull toward her, it disconcerted him. He hadn't even looked at women since Sherry died.

Melanie Carlotti's eyes are blue, like Sherry's.

Sherry.

He still thought about his wife and the argument they'd had the night of her accident fourteen months ago. It was impossible for him to stop thinking about it. When she died, his world had fallen apart, and he'd been trying to rebuild it ever since—working long hours, feeling restless, spending time with Amy, wishing for the past. Still, when Melanie Carlotti had walked into his office…

He considered how Amy had run to her. Flo had been right about Amy never going to strangers. She was usually shy with anyone she didn't know.

When the elevator door opened onto the fourth floor, Melanie stepped out. He couldn't keep himself from studying her as she walked to the reception area.

There was something about her that made his heart pound and his blood surge. He usually appreciated long hair on women, but Melanie's short, layered light brown hair had a slight wave that framed her face so naturally. The sunlight shining through the plate-glass windows caught blond strands. Her pearl earrings matched the buttons on her dress. He was glad to see she wasn't wearing high heels. The low pumps were stylish and more suitable for touring offices that weren't yet finished.

Zack led her through the fourth floor amid workmen who were spackling drywall, and her light perfume teased him. When they paused in the area that would be his office suite, he felt as if he were awakening from a long sleep, noticing curves on a woman again—the curves on Melanie Carlotti.

She gazed out the windows, admiring the view, the mountains in the distance. The late-October sunlight danced off the redwoods, oaks whose leaves were turning yellow and the madrones with their reddish bark. "It's beautiful here," she said softly.

Crossing to the window, he stood beside her. "That's why I built here. I wanted to get out of the city."

"I don't blame you." Her gaze went to the mountains again. "Just being able to look out at all of this would make coming to work a pleasure."

They were standing close, and he could sense she really understood why he'd moved his headquarters. He noticed that she wore lipstick but no other makeup. Her skin looked so very soft.

He found himself confiding, "I have to remind myself often that there's a blue sky out there, mountain peaks and more to my life than work."

Melanie faced him then, and he had the feeling she was absorbing not only the surroundings but everything he said and how he said it.

"I imagine your daughter helps to do that, too."

"She's one of the reasons I work so hard. I think about her while I'm working. That's why eventually I'd like to add a day care center here. If my staff can have their kids on-site, they won't worry so much about them."

"That's a great idea," Melanie murmured, but then she glanced outside again. Before she did, he saw so much emotion in her blue eyes that he wondered what it was all about. As she moved away from the windows, he thought maybe he'd imagined it.

A half hour later they'd toured all four floors and stood in what would be the main lobby of the building. Zack looked at her expectantly as she admired the vaulted ceiling with its skylight. "Ideas?"

She took a deep breath. "I'd use Australian pine flooring in your office suite along with specialty rugs, carpet in all the reception areas, parquet in the executive office suites." Motioning to the view through the windows, she added, "I'd try to bring the outside in. If you wait here, I'll show you exactly what I have in mind."

Before he could blink, she was gone.

A few minutes later when she came through the revolving front door, her arms were stacked with three huge sample books. He hurried to help her.

As soon as she was through the door, he reached out to take the books from her. The back of his hand brushed her waist and the underside of her breast. As he took the heavy books into his arms, a jolt of electric arousal ran through him. When his gaze collided with hers, her cheeks grew very pink.

"Let's put them over on the sawhorses," she murmured, and the lightning moment of awareness faded but didn't vanish.

Bending over the stack of books, she quickly opened the top one and leafed through it. He was looking over her shoulder, and with every breath he inhaled her delicate perfume. Leaving the book open, she pulled the second one out from under it and paged through that one, finally showing him wallpaper and fabric samples in teal, blue and tan.

"I'd build around these." When she glanced at him, her face was very near his. For a moment she seemed to lose her train of thought, but then she took a breath and quickly continued, "I'd use camel leather, hunter-green accessories, off-white to accent. We could go with a theme color for each floor and tie them all together in your reception area."

He found himself fascinated by this woman, who seemed chock-full of energy and ideas, as well as confidence.

But before he could respond to her suggestions, his cell phone rang. Taking it from his belt he said, "Excuse me. I'm expecting a call from one of my store managers." When he stepped away from her, he attempted to give his full attention to the call.

Closing the sample books, Melanie felt her heart pound as she waited for Zack to finish his conversation. Had she made a good impression? Were her ideas what he wanted?

A few minutes later he looked troubled as he closed the cell phone and hooked it onto his belt. "I have to leave."

She didn't want the interview to end like this without any resolution. "Do you want me to meet you back here again later?"

"No."

From the tone of Zachary Morgan's voice, Melanie was afraid she'd read him wrong. If she didn't get this job, how was she going to—

"You obviously know what you're doing," Zack said. "And I can tell that you have a feel for what I want to do here. The truth is, I'm on a tight schedule.

Our grand opening isn't until January second, but I need the offices finished before Christmas. You've got the job if you want it. If you come back here tomorrow morning, you can sign your contract and get started.''

Melanie was speechless for a good two seconds, then she recovered. ''That's wonderful!'' Her enthusiasm covered much more than simply the job offer. ''I can't wait to start.''

His gaze studied her appraisingly. ''Those medical problems you spoke of. Are you sure you're recovered? These deadlines are important, and if there's any chance you can't finish the work...'' He looked concerned. ''That would put me in a real bind.''

''I'm fine. Really,'' she assured him. ''Nothing will keep me from working and finishing the job.''

''All right, then. Now about the salary.'' He named a wage that was more than fair.

''That sounds just right.'' She'd already decided any salary would do if it enabled her to get the answers she needed.

''It's a deal, then,'' he said with a smile, extending his hand.

When she placed her hand in Zack's, there was that electric contact again—an awareness that she was a woman and he was a man. Then, suddenly, a barrier went up in Zachary Morgan's eyes.

He released her and stepped away. ''I'll carry these out to your car for you.''

As Zack stacked the books, easily gathered them up and strode to the revolving door, Melanie followed him, overjoyed she'd gotten the job but nervous about what came next.

At her car he asked, ''Back seat or trunk?''

''Trunk,'' she answered, unlocking it with her key.

When it popped open, he set the books on top of other catalogs and samples that were stacked alongside her folded drafting table. "You came prepared."

"It's not unusual for a client to ask for preliminary ideas."

After he closed the trunk, they stood there for a moment under the autumn sun, a slight breeze ruffling their hair. Neither of them seemed to have anything to say, yet they both seemed reluctant to end the interview.

Finally Zack asked, "Can you be here at 9:00 a.m.?"

She nodded, and then she used her remote to unlock the car door. So many feelings were bubbling inside of her, and she didn't know what any of them meant. Underneath all of them was a sense of something unfinished, something important. A goal she had to reach. First she had to find out what it was.

Zack walked with her and opened the driver's door. As he stood towering above her, the urge to touch him was so strong she had to curl her fingers into her palm. He seemed to lean closer for just a moment. She looked at his lips and wondered what a kiss from him would be like. Then he straightened.

She gave herself a mental shake and slid into the bucket seat.

His hand rested on the car door. "I'll see you tomorrow morning."

She nodded, tore her gaze reluctantly from his and inserted the key into the ignition. He closed her door.

When she drove out of the parking lot of Sports & More, Inc., she glanced into her rearview mirror. Zachary Morgan was staring after her. The thought made her nervous and excited at the same time, and she wished tomorrow morning wasn't so far away.

* * *

As Melanie typed up preliminary plans for Zack Morgan's offices on her laptop computer in the motel room that evening, she was suddenly uncertain about accepting Zack's job offer. When he found out why she was really here, would he feel betrayed? Would he feel as if she'd duped him somehow?

Yet she didn't know what she could do differently. This job was a wonderful opportunity to find out what type of woman Sherry Morgan had been and why she seemed to be calling to her…to have something to say that Melanie couldn't decipher.

She had no doubts that if she told Zack why she was actually here, he'd want nothing to do with her.

Still in turmoil, in spite of her reasoning and her decision to go forward with her plan, she became aware of cars pulling up outside. Voices. Trunks opening and closing. The motel only had fifteen rooms, and parking spaces were right outside the doors. There was a restaurant and bar across the street where she'd bought herself a salad and a sandwich. But as she'd sat at the small Formica table, she'd worked on notes and had left half of the sandwich uneaten.

Now comfortably settled against the headboard of the bed, she adjusted her reading glasses and concentrated on the notes she'd made. Dusk was dimming to darkness, and she turned on the bedside lamp so she could see more clearly.

Around ten o'clock she heard a commotion outside and glanced out the window. A group of men, at least twenty of them, had crossed the street to the motel, laughing, talking and clapping each other on the back. Under the parking lot light she could tell that a few of them weren't too steady on their feet, and she suspected they'd been drinking. Going over to her door, she attached the chain lock and then closed the draperies.

The men grew rowdier. She heard someone outside her door ask, "I wonder who's holed up in here? Maybe they'd like to come out and join the party." There was a sharp banging on her door. Anxiety gripped the pit of Melanie's stomach.

When the banging started again, she wasn't sure what to do. She was relieved when she heard a second man's voice say, "Come on, Chet. Let's go have some beer and watch TV."

Their voices became a low rumble as motel doors opened and shut.

But a half hour later, Melanie could hardly think because the TV in the room next door was blasting so loud. Once more she heard men's voices outside. Not just two, but three or four or five. She couldn't make out exactly what was going on, but there was swearing and the sound of something heavy banging on metal. She saved the work she'd finished on her computer just as a loud thump sounded—as if someone had been thrown against her door. After a few shouts, a six-pack came crashing through her window, shattering the glass.

The sound of the breaking glass made her freeze, and memories of the night of the fire flooded her mind. She began trembling as all of it played through her head vividly…harshly…indelibly—the knock on her neighbor's door where Melanie was attending a Christmas party, the mad dash to her own house, the smoke seeping from under the eaves, the flash of fire in the living room. She'd grasped the hot doorknob. Her world exploded, glass shattering everywhere….

She was caught up in all of it again until sirens pulled her back into the present. Suddenly flashing lights appeared in the parking lot, and Melanie heard the sound of authoritative voices.

She hardly had time to slide her computer onto the bed before there was a knock at her door. "Miss?" a deep voice called. "It's the police. I've got the manager with me. Are you all right?"

Fortunately, she'd been sitting on the bed tucked into the corner by the wall. Slipping off her glasses and sidestepping the shattered glass, she crossed to the door and opened it with the chain lock still attached. She could see the blue-uniformed officer, and he was holding up his badge.

Her hands were shaking as she unfastened the lock and pulled the door open.

The officer gave her a quick, thorough appraisal. "Any of that glass hit you?"

"No, I'm fine." At least she would be fine if she could stop shaking.

"You're Melanie Carlotti?"

The manager must have given the officer her name. "Yes. What happened?"

"A group of good ol' boys decided to attend the festival at Clear Lake without their wives. It turns out they obviously don't know how to behave without them. They've battered up a few of the rooms as well as each other. We're taking them in, although the ones who aren't in trouble are still staying here tonight. The problem is—you can't stay in this room, and nothing else is available."

She glanced at the broken window. "Do you have any suggestions?"

"Unfortunately, motels around here are pretty booked up. You'll either have to go up ahead about an hour or back to Santa Rosa."

She didn't know her way around Santa Rosa. She'd only ever passed through the town. Glancing at her watch, she saw it was almost eleven. She had a nine-o'clock appointment with Zachary Morgan. Maybe the best thing to do was to call him and let him know she had to change locations. Maybe he could recommend a place to stay and how to get there.

"I need to make a phone call, Officer."

"Go ahead. I'm going to be putting the fear of God into the fellows who are staying here tonight. Take your time."

Crossing to the phone, she sat on the bed and pulled out the sheet of stationery that had detailed the time and place of her interview today. The phone number was on the letterhead. If it was the phone number for Zack Morgan's offices... All she could do was try. She dialed quickly and hoped for at least an answering machine.

Instead of an answering machine, a deep male voice answered. "Morgan here."

"Mr. Morgan. It's Melanie Carlotti. I'm sorry to be calling you so late."

"No problem. I'm still working. What can I do for you?"

She hesitated, then explained, "I need to relocate. I can't stay in the motel at Cool Ridge tonight. There was a brawl, and the police are here."

"Are you all right?"

"I'm fine, but the window to my room was shattered, and—"

"You're sure you're all right?" he asked again, sounding concerned.

"Yes. Really. The reason I'm calling... I'm not familiar with Santa Rosa. Can you recommend a place to stay? Maybe even a guest house, rather than a motel.''

There was silence on the other end of the line until Zack decided, ''I don't think it's a good idea for you to go driving around yourself at this time of night.''

''Oh, I don't mind that. It would just be helpful if I knew where I was going.''

Again a pensive silence. Finally he said, ''It would be even more helpful if you knew you were safe for the night. Why don't you come and stay at my penthouse?''

Melanie stared at the phone in stunned silence.

Stay at Zachary Morgan's penthouse? The idea intrigued her as well as scared her. From her investigator's report, from her own sense of the man, she believed Zack Morgan had integrity and she'd be safe with him. Spending the night with him could create an atmosphere where she could get closer to him.

Is that truly what she wanted?

Chapter Two

"Melanie?" Zack Morgan asked.

"I'm here." Her mind was spinning with all the possibilities of getting to know him better. "I don't want to be a bother."

"You won't be. Mrs. Briggs has the guest room made up. It's in the wing with her quarters, on the other side of the penthouse from mine, so if you're worried about impropriety, don't be. She's an adequate chaperone."

A chaperone. That eased her mind a bit. Still...

"I don't know—"

"I feel responsible for you, since you came here to accept a job I'm offering. I'm just glad I had my calls forwarded from my office or I wouldn't have gotten yours."

She thought about a drive back to Santa Rosa. She thought about her early appointment with Zack. She thought about her purpose for being here in the first place. What better way to find some answers than to stay under his roof?

Glancing at the broken window and at the glass on the floor, she realized she was still shaken by the whole incident. "Your offer's very kind. I don't know if the police will want to talk to me again, but—"

"Sit tight. I'll be there in fifteen minutes to pick you up."

"Oh, but you don't have to—" Then she heard a click and realized that Zack had already hung up. He was a man of action, and apparently once he got an idea into his head, nothing changed his course.

By the time Melanie spoke to the policeman again and repacked the few things that she'd unpacked, Zack pulled into the parking lot in a shiny, black SUV. He climbed out, saw her outside her motel room door and strode toward her. Casually dressed now in a tan, collarless knit shirt, his shoulders looked even broader than they had in his white shirt. His blue jeans fit like a pair of jeans should, and Melanie couldn't believe the direction of her thoughts in the midst of the situation she was in.

There had been an attraction between her and Phil— enough to make that part of their marriage satisfying. But Phil's devil-may-care attitude toward life had interfered with that sometimes, too. There hadn't been a passionate intensity, and sometimes she felt that Phil didn't care whether he made love with her or not. She was still so furious at him sometimes for being so careless, for not remembering to unplug the Christmas tree lights....

Thoughts of her husband fled as Zack moved in front of her. He greeted the burly policeman standing beside her, then studied her. "Are you sure you're all right?"

She nodded and introduced him to the officer.

"Can she leave now?" Zack asked him.

"She sure can. She's a tough little lady. Many women I know would have become hysterical at what happened here."

"That wouldn't have done any good," Melanie murmured, embarrassed.

"Is your luggage still in your room?" Zack asked. "I'll put it in the car."

The officer moved away then, toward the manager of the motel who was standing by one of the cruisers.

Melanie looked up at Zack. "Mr. Morgan, I can get my own luggage and drive myself to your headquarters. You didn't have to drive all the way out here."

"It's Zack," he said. "I don't think you should drive after what happened."

She'd been shaken by the six-pack soaring through the window and by a return of memories she couldn't forget. Now she was steadier. "I'm going to need my car tomorrow. I don't want to inconvenience you any more than I have. There's absolutely no reason why I shouldn't drive myself."

Zack remembered how upset Sherry had been the night of their argument...the night of her accident. He should have kept her from driving away. But he hadn't. Maybe that's why he'd raced out here. If Melanie was upset, he didn't want her driving. Yet she didn't look upset. She looked perfectly calm, and he realized she had an independent streak like Sherry's. Except Sherry's independence had sometimes been based on selfishness. In fact, she'd been so selfish she'd wanted to abort their child. If she'd lived, he didn't think he could have ever forgiven her for that.

"All right," he concluded, "you can follow me. But

there's no reason I shouldn't at least take your luggage. Unless you're afraid I'm going to drive away with it.''

She laughed, and he was surprised at how satisfied he felt that he had brought a smile to her face. Then he picked up her suitcase and garment bag and carried them to his car.

Less than a half hour later, Zack led Melanie toward the back entrance of the parking lot, put down his window and motioned her to follow him into the four-car garage. Once her car had pulled up next to his, he lowered the door with his remote, then met her at the elevator. She was carrying her laptop computer, and she looked tired.

''Long day?'' he asked, as the doors to the elevator slid open.

''Just one with lots of...excitement,'' she said with a small smile.

''Uh-oh. I'm afraid you're putting the job to decorate my offices in the same category as having a six-pack thrown through your motel room window.'' He wanted to lighten her mood, and it was an odd feeling wanting to do that for somebody. He teased his daughter, of course, but with everyone else he'd been much too serious for a very long time.

''You'd think I'd be old enough to expect life's unexpected turns.''

The doors slid shut and they were alone in the silent, dimly lit elevator. An intimacy seemed to surround them that came from the late night, the cocoonlike feeling of being in an elevator car, the knowledge that they'd be working closely together for a few months.

''I'm not sure anyone gets used to that,'' Zack said.

She looked up at him then, and he saw a knowing in her eyes. But that was impossible. She couldn't know he had gone through major unexpected turns in his life, too.

When the elevator slid smoothly to a stop, the doors swished open and Zack led her across the hall to the penthouse. He took out his key and unlocked the door. "I told Flo she didn't have to wait up for us."

Yet, when they stepped inside, lights were blazing in both the living room and kitchen, and he could immediately see why. His housekeeper sat at the kitchen table and his daughter was in the high chair with a sip-it cup.

He set down Melanie's luggage and went over to them, lifting Amy out of her chair. "What are you doing up?"

Flo shook her head. "This one's going to be a night owl like you. Five minutes after you left, she woke up and wanted to play. And you know I can't stand to see her cry."

Flo could be firm with Amy when she had to be. But she also had a soft heart, and Amy knew just how to get to her. She knew how to get to him, too. Her little hands came up to his cheeks, and she said, "Da-dee," with a smile that lit up everything about his life.

He sensed that Melanie didn't know whether she should come into the kitchen or wait for him in the living room. Trying to put her at ease, he asked, "Would you like something to drink or eat? Flo always has a jar full of cookies."

After only a slight hesitation, Melanie came farther into the kitchen and nodded at Flo. "I'm sorry I disrupted everyone's night."

"Nonsense," Flo said with a smile. "This isn't the first night Amy's decided she doesn't want to sleep. Zack told me what happened at the motel. You didn't get hurt, did you?"

Melanie shook her head.

Zack noticed that Melanie's gaze kept shifting toward his daughter, and suddenly Amy leaned away from his arms and held her hands out to Melanie.

"Is it all right if I hold her?" Melanie asked Zack.

"Sure." He was again surprised that his daughter had made a new friend so easily.

When Melanie took Amy into her arms, the little girl snuggled on her shoulder and with a yawn, closed her eyes.

"Well, doesn't that beat all!" Flo said. "I've been trying to get her to do that for the last half hour."

Zack couldn't take his gaze off Melanie and the expression on her face as she held his daughter. He noticed how she smoothed the hair over Amy's ear. Her eyes were so full of emotion that he almost felt as if he were intruding on a private moment. That was ridiculous.

Five minutes later, after Flo took Amy to her room, Zack led Melanie to the guest bedroom and realized it looked very sparse. He hadn't hired a decorator to furnish the penthouse. He'd simply gone to a furniture store, picked out groupings and what he thought he needed. This bedroom had no window coverings since privacy wasn't an issue. It also didn't have any area rugs on the bare wood floor. The distressed pine furniture was big and bulky, and Melanie looked fragile and delicate in the surroundings. She'd already proved she wasn't either.

Setting down her luggage, he commented, "The offices are my main priority but if you have some time, maybe you could warm up the penthouse, too. I bought everything we thought we needed, but the furniture doesn't fill it and something's definitely missing."

Melanie put her computer on the long dresser. "I'd be glad to help you with the penthouse."

"Even Amy's room can use livening up. When we moved here a few weeks ago, I left behind everything from her old room." It had been good for him to leave the house where he'd lived with Sherry...where he wasn't bumping into a memory in every room.

"Did you like living in Santa Rosa?"

She must have assumed he'd lived there since that's where his old headquarters were located. "It's a nice town, but after my wife died, I decided I needed a change, too. Living above my office will be convenient."

Knowing he should say good-night, he had the oddest reluctance to leave Melanie. He was curious to know more about her. He could still smell the lingering scent of her perfume. In her pale peach sweatsuit she looked warm and cuddly. The rise of her breasts under the soft knit shirt drew his gaze. The urge to hold her in his arms, kiss her and touch her was so strong he felt like a teenager again.

But he was her employer and there was no room in his life for a woman. He put some distance between them. "Sometimes Amy wakes up crying in the middle of the night. Don't be alarmed. Either Flo or I will take care of her."

"But you sleep in another wing?"

"Yes. Next to my office. I have a monitor in my bedroom as well as in the office, so I know if she's awake."

Melanie walked with him to the door, but he stopped when they reached it. "Don't hesitate to ask if you need something. Flo told me she put out fresh towels for you. She usually has breakfast for us around eight. If you want to catch more sleep, don't feel you have to join us.''

''I'm an early riser. Once I've had that first cup of coffee, then I'm ready for the day.''

Unbidden, Zack remembered that Sherry hadn't been a morning person at all. She'd hated that 5:00 a.m. feeding with a passion. But then, he wasn't sure exactly how much she had enjoyed their infant daughter. He'd hoped…

His hopes didn't matter anymore.

After he stepped out into the hall, Melanie said, ''Mr. Morgan, I want to—''

''Zack,'' he corrected her again quickly.

''Zack,'' she repeated softly. ''Thanks again for rescuing me tonight.''

Shaking his head, he grimaced. ''Don't confuse me with a white knight. They all fell off their horses decades ago. Get a good night's sleep. I'll see you in the morning.''

As Zack strode down the hall, he heard Melanie's door close, and an idea took hold of him. He'd sleep on it.

The next morning Zack sat in his office and underlined the number of the last reference on Melanie's résumé. He'd hired Melanie because her professional reputation was sterling. Job applicants usually suggested references who would say good things about them. Yet if an employer asked the right questions, he could figure out how long the references had known the applicant and what they really felt. Melanie's clients not only liked her work, they obviously liked *her*. But now Zack had an idea that could possibly help the work on his offices get finished faster.

From everything he'd seen of Melanie, she was a decent, caring woman. He'd gotten the idea from her clients that when she took on their jobs she became more than their decorator—she became their friend. Still, a man couldn't be too careful, and that's why he wanted to talk to Melanie's personal reference. He picked up his phone, hoping this final reference was an early riser.

A few minutes later he was speaking to Barbara Adair, whom Melanie had listed as a friend.

"How long have you and Melanie been friends?" Zack asked, after an introduction and a few preliminary questions.

"Almost seven years," Barbara responded. "We were neighbors."

Zack waited, but when she didn't add anything else he prompted her. "I know Melanie had medical problems. Do you think they'll interfere with her job performance?"

"Absolutely not," the woman returned vehemently. "Melanie has come through a difficult time with the kind of strength I wish I had."

Again Melanie's friend didn't go into specifics, but Zack could respect that. The admiring tone in Barbara Adair's voice told him even more than her words. Still, he had one more important question that had nothing to do with coordinating wallpaper and fabrics. "Can you tell me how well Melanie relates to children?"

There was a lengthy silence, and Zack supposed that was because the question seemed to come from left field. Then Barbara answered it. "She's wonderful with children. I've trusted my two with her often. My daughters stayed with her a few evenings a week while I worked part-time. And my older daughter, who's eight, prefers to go shopping with Melanie because she knows what's *cool*."

Real affection filled Barbara's voice, and Zack realized he had all the information he needed. After a few more cursory questions, along with thanks to Melanie's friend for taking time to answer his inquiries, he hung up the phone.

When he reached the kitchen, Amy was already in her high chair, and Flo was standing at the stove scrambling eggs. "Is Melanie up yet?" he asked his housekeeper.

"She let me take my shower first so I could start breakfast."

"What do you think of her?"

"I spent some time talking to her last night before we turned in. She seems very nice. Why?"

"Because I'm thinking about inviting her to stay here. That way she can take her time finding an apartment. With her on-site, maybe she can avert disasters before they happen."

"I see. You want her here for purely practical reasons," Flo said, her green eyes twinkling.

"Of course. What other reason would there be?"

"What other reason, indeed?" Flo muttered as she stirred the eggs. "The idea's fine with me."

"If it's too much extra work for you…"

"Nonsense. Feeding one more is never extra work. My guess is she'll be so involved with this project, I'll see her about as much as I see you."

Flo had given him the "your life has to be more than work" lecture more than once.

Just then, Melanie appeared in the doorway in a sky-blue pantsuit and flat shoes. "Good morning," she said with a shy smile.

There was a softness about her that he found so very appealing. He was used to dealing with harder-edged career women.

"Good morning." He went over to the coffeepot and quickly poured two mugs of coffee, remembering what she'd said about starting her day. He handed her one of them.

"Thank you." Her gaze locked to his, and he felt his heart starting to pound faster.

Flo cleared her throat loudly. "Breakfast is ready."

When they were all seated and Amy was stuffing bits of scrambled egg into her mouth, Zack took a sip of his coffee and then set it down. "There's something I'd like to discuss with you, Melanie."

"About your project?"

"About where you're going to be staying."

She laid her fork beside her plate. "I thought I'd go to the chamber of commerce in Santa Rosa and see if they have any information on guest houses. Maybe over the weekend I can contact a real estate agent about finding an apartment."

Leaning back in his chair, he suggested casually, "It might be good not to rush into that until you know the area better. How would you like to stay here until you find something you really want?"

Melanie's eyes widened in surprise as she looked from him to Flo, and he guessed what she was thinking. "Flo and I have already discussed this."

"I wouldn't want to impose—"

Flo waved her hand at Melanie. "It would be nice to have another adult around here to talk to." She gave Zack a mock scowl.

"What Flo is trying to say is that I'm hardly ever here. When I am, I'm either in my office or playing with Amy. This is really a selfish invitation on my part. I want my staff moved into these offices by January 2. You know how difficult it will be to get finished by then. If you're on the premises and don't have a morning and evening commute, you can consult with workmen anytime, and they can ask you questions since you'll be available. We'll avoid costly mistakes that way. What do you think?'' He watched her carefully as she thought about it.

"You might be right,'' she finally decided. "The project would be easier for all of us. And I'd love to have some time to look around Santa Rosa and pick out an area where I'd like to live, without rushing into anything.'' Melanie's gaze fell on Amy.

His daughter had been in the process of stuffing a bite of toast into her mouth. She stopped, stared back at Melanie, broke into a wide smile, then gave a happy little wave with her toast.

"Amy can get pretty noisy at times,'' he warned. "Will that bother you?''

"No,'' Melanie said softly. "Being around Amy will be a joy, not a bother.''

From the way Melanie said it, Zack could tell she really meant it. "I'm glad that's settled. Let's finish breakfast, then we'll go to my office and sign your contract.''

As Zack picked up his fork to dig into his eggs, he told himself he'd done the best thing to keep this project on schedule and his life running smoothly.

Sitting at her drafting table in Zack's guest bedroom, Melanie heard squeals from Amy and couldn't help taking off her glasses and putting her work aside. Her eyes still became tired sometimes. But she was so grateful to have her sight back.

When she'd awakened in the hospital after the fire and explosion to find her eyes bandaged, Dr. Jordan Wilson had first told her her husband and little girl were dead. Before she could absorb that loss, he'd also gently informed her that her corneas had been damaged by shattered glass.

She'd had to wait nine months for her eyes to heal enough for her to have corneal transplants. If it hadn't been for her best friend Barbara inviting her to stay with her family, Melanie knew she couldn't have coped as well as she had. After surgery, it had taken another year for her sight to improve enough for her to simply need reading glasses. Jordan had performed the surgery and become her friend. Regaining her eyesight was still such a miracle to her.

Leaving her room, she headed toward Amy's laughter. The day had seemed to pass in a spin—finalizing her contract with Zack, studying the floor plans of his offices and examining each inch of space with an eye on her sample books. She'd only seen Zack for a short while this morning. He'd left for Santa Rosa after their meeting and hadn't returned, as far as she knew. She still couldn't believe she was staying in his penthouse! When he'd first proposed the idea, she'd panicked. Then she'd realized if Sherry Morgan was calling to her in some other-worldly way, this was the place where she could figure it out.

Amy's giggles were coming from the bathroom. When Flo heard Melanie's footsteps, she called, "Can you grab me another bath towel from the linen closet? I forgot to bring an extra one in."

Melanie fetched the towel, feeling altogether com-

fortable with Flo Briggs. They'd fixed supper together—salads and a stir-fry. Apparently, Zack had
called Flo to tell her he wouldn't be home for supper.
The woman had clucked over Zack working too hard
and not eating right and had admitted to Melanie that
she'd come to think of Zack as the son she'd never had.

Melanie pulled a fluffy pink towel from the closet
and took it into the bathroom. She couldn't help going
over to the bathtub and kneeling beside it, thinking of
all the times she'd bathed her daughter. Kaitlyn had
loved the water. It seemed as if Amy did, too, as she
sat in the tub and splashed as much as she could. A
stream of water hit the front of Melanie's T-shirt,
quickly followed by a second stream that splashed onto
her jeans.

Flo started, "I'm sorry she—"

Melanie laughed. "This is what toddlers do in the
bathtub. I always—" She stopped.

Flo gave her an odd look.

She was kept from having to continue or explain by
Zack's appearance in the doorway. "Is this a party?"

Drops of water flew onto Melanie's cheek as Amy
splashed and giggled. She brushed them away. "A
splash party."

Smiling, Zack came into the small room. After he
tugged his tie down and opened the top button at his
collar, he noticed the front of Melanie's T-shirt. The
laughter left his eyes, replaced by something
deeper…something fiery that excited Melanie, yet made
her feel a little bit afraid, too. Neither of them spoke
for a few moments. Neither of them looked away.

Then Flo said to Amy, "Come on, poppet, let's get
you out of the water."

But when she reached for the little girl, Amy shook her head insistently and splashed some more.

"Now," Flo said firmly.

After glancing at Flo, Amy looked at Melanie, and without hesitation reached her arms out to her.

Melanie wasn't sure what to do, but Flo merely sat back on her haunches. "She's taken a shine to you."

Melanie's throat tightened, and she didn't know if the feelings she had toward this little girl were hers or if they belonged to Sherry Morgan. She only knew she couldn't turn away from her—that she had to hold her.

Taking the towel from the rim of the bathtub, Melanie opened it and scooped Amy up into her arms.

Amy reached out and touched a lock of Melanie's hair, then smiled at her. Melanie knew some people believed that children could talk to the angels. Could Amy sense her mother's spirit?

Melanie took a deep breath, feeling as if she were an explorer in uncharted territory. "I'll take her to her room."

As Melanie passed Zack, she was aware of his chest only inches from her...aware of his attention on her. She didn't look at him. She couldn't. He might see something in her eyes she didn't want him to see.

After she set Amy on her changing table, Zack came up beside her. "I'll take over now. She and I haven't spent any time together today."

Melanie had started to step away when Amy reached for her. "Your daddy's going to put you to bed," Melanie explained with a smile.

But Amy just stared at Melanie, her lower lip trembling, and she reached out her arms again.

"It looks as if she wants you to do the honors tonight," Zack said quietly.

"What would you like me to do?" Melanie finally looked up at him.

He held up a disposable diaper. "Do you know how to use one of these?"

"I think I can figure it out," she responded with a smile. Kaitlyn had gone through disposable diapers until shortly after her second birthday.

Together she and Zack got Amy ready for bed. Melanie's fingers trembled as she fastened the snaps on Amy's pj's. Then she picked her up and set her in her crib.

Amy looked up at Zack. "BoBo."

He chuckled. "Right. We can't forget BoBo." He picked up a stuffed blue donkey sitting in the corner of the rocking chair and gave it to his daughter. With a grin at both of them, Amy tucked the donkey under her arm and lay on her side on the mattress, poking her thumb into her mouth.

"Good night," Zack whispered as he leaned down and kissed her cheek.

"Good night, Amy," Melanie said softly, wishing she had the right to kiss the little girl as Zack had done. She felt tears burn in her eyes, and a wealth of sadness washed over her with them. The turmoil like a squall inside of her was more than grief. She quickly turned away from Zack and headed toward her bedroom.

"I'm going to turn in now," she murmured over her shoulder.

But he caught up with her outside of her door. "Melanie."

She stopped, composed herself as best she could, and turned to face him.

"I won't let Amy take advantage of you."

"Oh, she isn't."

"If she thinks she can get away with it, she will. All she has to do is smile at me and I'm jumping through hoops."

Melanie felt her heart lighten as she gazed at this strong, confident, self-directed man who could admit his little girl had power over him. "You're her daddy. All *I* had to do was smile at my dad, and I could get that extra piece of chocolate or stay out later. That's the way it's supposed to be."

"Where are your parents now?" Zack asked her.

"I lost my dad when I was fourteen, and Mom the year after I graduated from college." She'd lost so many people she'd loved. Sometimes she wondered why.

"I'm sorry," Zack said.

She saw the pain in Zack's eyes and knew he was thinking about his own losses. She wished she could ask him what kind of marriage he'd had...what kind of person Sherry Morgan had been. It was too soon for that.

The shadowy hall seemed to hum—with feelings and memories and a connection to Zack that Melanie wondered if he could feel, too. Finally he motioned toward the kitchen. "I'd better get some supper. I have a few hours of work ahead of me."

"Flo made a plate for you that you can warm up in the microwave. There was salad left, too."

He nodded but didn't move away. He kept searching her face, as if he was looking for an answer to a question he didn't voice. When his gaze lingered on her lips, she felt her breath hitch and a shiver pass through her.

Taking a step back, he motioned to her T-shirt. "You'd better get changed."

She just nodded, longing to be held in his

arms...longing to feel his lips on hers...longing to know Zack Morgan in a very intimate way.

"I'll see you in the morning." His voice was husky, and that fire was back in his eyes.

"In the morning," Melanie repeated.

When Zack turned and walked away, Melanie wondered how he doused a fire like that. Did it smolder until it leaped into passionate flames?

Shaking her head, she went inside her room and closed the door, knowing fire was the last thing she needed. It had been a fire that had destroyed her life. Yet the fire in Zack Morgan drew her to him. She prayed it wouldn't destroy her life again.

Chapter Three

*W*hite and gray clouds swirled around the jagged mountain peak. Drizzling rain fell everywhere and it was so bone-chillingly cold. Melanie felt as if she were floating around the mountain along with the clouds and a pair of pink-and-blue baby booties. Suddenly she was still.

She peered through the drizzling rain. To the east of the mountain, Zack stood holding Amy, looking up toward the peak. To the west of the mountain stood a beautiful woman with long, curly, dark-brown hair. She wasn't looking up at the mountain peak. She was looking toward Melanie and beckoning to her. Melanie found she couldn't walk toward the woman. She was frozen in place, and panic rushed through her. She began to tremble, then she finally reached out her hand to Sherry Morgan…

Melanie's eyelids flew open and she sat up in bed. She was shaking and she was *so* cold. She knew it would take all night to get warm again. Sherry Morgan wanted something of her. But what?

Dropping her head into her hands, Melanie combed her fingers through her short hair. Maybe she was just going absolutely, stark-raving crazy. After she took a few deep breaths, she knew there was one way to decide that. She needed to see a picture of Zack's deceased wife.

Each hour ticked by slowly as sleep eluded Melanie and she waited for morning to come. When it did, she was relieved. She was also afraid. Even if she found the next part of the puzzle, where would it all lead?

She thought about Zack and last night and how she'd felt and what she'd wished. The longing to be held in his arms had been overwhelmingly strong. The yearning to be kissed by him had been a deep ache. Her ache...or Sherry Morgan's?

When Melanie went out to the kitchen, she was almost relieved to find that Zack had already eaten and gone. Amy smiled and waved and babbled something about BoBo and Daddy. Melanie wished she had the freedom to pick up the little girl and kiss her and hug her and say good morning as she would to her own child.

Flo glanced over her shoulder. "'Morning. Would you like me to scramble eggs for you? Zack had an early appointment in Santa Rosa so he took off."

"Just some coffee and toast is fine."

Over breakfast Melanie and Flo chatted about Clear Lake and the entertainers that appeared there, until Amy began banging on her tray—she wanted out of her high chair.

Flo shook her head and laughed. "This one knows

exactly what she wants. She's got her dad's determination and Sherry's stubbornness.''

''Ah, but she inherited somebody's sweetness, too.'' Melanie was positive of that.

''I suppose that's the best part of both Zack *and* Sherry.''

''Did you know Sherry well?''

''I've known Zack since he was a kid, and I got to know Sherry after they married. I was a neighbor of his dad's. After my husband died, I was at loose ends. Then Zack lost Sherry, and I offered to take care of Amy until he found someone. But I loved doing it, and six months ago I sold my house and moved in with him. It's worked out great. And now I love being out here with the mountains and all.''

As Flo wiped Amy's face, Melanie asked as casually as possible, ''Does Amy look more like Zack or more like her mother?''

Flo thought about it. ''That's a good question. Probably about half and half of each. There's a picture of Sherry and Zack in the corner cupboard in the living room. Go take a peek.''

Melanie went into the living room and headed straight for the corner cupboard. There stood a five-by-seven photo of Zack and a beautiful brunette. She hadn't noticed it before. Or had she? Sherry Morgan was definitely the woman who'd beckoned to her in her dream.

Melanie wondered if she'd subconsciously seen this picture when she was in the living room. She hadn't been in here much, and she couldn't remember noticing it. That didn't mean she hadn't.

She took a few moments to steady herself, then went back to the kitchen. ''I think you're right. Half and half.'' Feeling more than a little off balance, she said, ''I have to make some calls before I go downstairs to the offices.'' She took the cordless phone from the counter in the kitchen. ''If you need this, just come and get it.''

''Oh, I won't be needing that. I'm going to mix up some oatmeal cookies if this little scamp will let me.''

Amy grinned in delight. ''Cook—ies.''

Melanie felt a stab of remembrance of her little girl asking for the treat in exactly the same way. She left the kitchen with the phone, hurried to her bedroom and closed the door.

She had to call a few suppliers, but first she needed to talk to Jordan. Maybe he could help her make sense of all this. Would he still be at home or at the hospital? Jordan Wilson might be her ophthalmologist, but more important, he was her friend. She decided to try him at home first.

When he picked up on the second ring, she let out a relieved breath. ''Jordan, it's Melanie.''

''I've been worried about you.''

She'd told Jordan all about her plans to meet Zachary Morgan. ''Everything's gotten a little complicated. He hired me and I'm staying at his penthouse.''

''You're what?''

''Don't start fretting, Jordan. His housekeeper's room is next to mine. She and his daughter are great chaperones.''

''Does Morgan know who you are?'' Her friend's voice was worried.

''No, I can't tell him that yet. He'd think I was crazy. You know he would.''

''*I* didn't think you were crazy.''

''That's different. You were my doctor.''

"I'm an ophthalmologist who's never heard of the kind of experiences you're having."

"You have an open mind."

"You didn't give me much choice."

She smiled at that. "That's not true and you know it. You're an understanding man, Jordan, and that made it easy for me to confide in you. I haven't told anyone else about any of this except for Barbara. You know that. I still can't. I can't take the chance that Zack Morgan will shut me out of his life if he thinks I'm loony."

"I'm sure he'll be able to tell you're not loony," Jordan returned with some amusement now.

"I don't know. Sometimes none of it makes any sense to me, either. There's this connection I feel toward his daughter, too. And I had this dream last night..." Her voice trailed off.

"I'm afraid you're going to get hurt," he said quietly.

Even though he couldn't see her, she shook her head. "I can't hurt any more than I have since the fire. I really have no choice in this. I'll never have peace of mind until I figure it all out."

"I suppose you won't. Just remember, you can pull out any time, and you can call me if you need me."

Jordan was in his midforties and, more than anything else, he'd been like an older brother to her. When she'd first confided in him about what was happening, they'd had long discussions on life and death and everything in between. They'd had lunches and a few dinners and he'd become a very special friend.

"Thank you for seeing me through all of this," she murmured. "I don't know what I would have done without you."

"Your friendship means a lot to me, too. It made me

realize there's more to life than hospitals and patients and science. You've helped me to remember again there are things we can't explain and maybe we shouldn't. Keep that in mind, okay?''

"Okay.''

After she hung up, she knew she had to understand as much as she could or she wouldn't be able to move forward in her life.

The following afternoon Melanie stopped in at the penthouse to get some papers with specifications for the offices. There was a note on the refrigerator from Flo that said she'd taken Amy out in her stroller. Melanie was surprised by the thought that she'd rather be out with Flo and Amy than working. She'd poured her life into her work since she'd recovered from the accident, but now her work just didn't seem as important as spending time with that little girl. Sherry's feelings or her own?

Going to the refrigerator, she took out a carton of orange juice and poured herself a glass. Time to immerse herself in work and stop thinking about all of it. She was headed back to the bedroom with her glass of juice when the phone rang. She knew there was a machine hooked up to it, but what if Zack was trying to reach her for some reason? He was on the road today, meeting with a distributor. He'd told her he wouldn't be back until after dinner.

Snatching up the handset, she answered it. "Zack Morgan's residence.''

"Hello?'' a woman's voice said. "Is this Mrs. Briggs?''

"No. My name is Melanie Carlotti. I work for Mr. Morgan.''

"Oh, I see. Well, I've left messages at all of his numbers. Can I leave another one with you? This is sort of urgent."

"Sure."

"I'm Mr. Morgan's real estate agent. A contract came in on his house, and it's a good one. But the buyer wants to take immediate possession and we need to get this settled. Could you have him give me a call as soon as possible?"

"If he checks in, I'll tell him. If not, I'll give him the message as soon as I see him this evening."

When Melanie hung up, she realized that with this move, Zack was putting his old life behind him...or at least he was trying to. She had the feeling his loss was still raw, and she wished she knew why. Because he'd loved his wife so much? Or was there something else? Something else that had to do with her dreams and Sherry beckoning to her.

Amy was already in bed by the time Zack came home that night. After stopping to greet Flo and Melanie, he went to his daughter's room to say good-night. By the time Zack had kissed Amy, Flo had set a plate of oatmeal cookies in the center of the kitchen table and gone to her room to watch TV.

Melanie waited in the kitchen for Zack, sipping a mug of tea. As soon as he entered the kitchen, she said, "I took a message for you from your real estate agent."

"I got it on the voice mail on my cell phone." He took a carton of milk from the refrigerator.

She pushed the mug away. "Has the house been on the market long?"

"About four months. I have to go through it tomorrow morning for the last time."

Melanie could only imagine how hard that would be.

Suddenly he looked at her and said, "Would you like to ride along and drive around Santa Rosa? We'll be back by noon."

Her heart beat faster. "Are you sure you want company? Letting go of the house where you lived is sometimes difficult."

He didn't respond right away but rather poured himself a glass of milk, took it over to the table and sat across from her. "It's just a house. Amy won't even remember it, and in a while I won't, either."

Could leaving the past behind really be easy for him? If she went into the house with him, would she feel Sherry's presence? She'd find out tomorrow. "I'd like to come with you."

"Can you be ready to leave after breakfast?"

"That's fine."

Zack reached for a cookie from the plate on the table, a faraway look in his eyes now.

No matter what he'd said, she suspected tonight he'd be thinking a lot about his marriage and the life he'd shared with his wife in the house, even if he didn't want to admit it.

Rising, she took her mug to the sink and then went to the doorway. "I'll see you in the morning."

When Zack nodded absently, she went to her room, wondering if she'd have another dream tonight, wondering what would happen if she told Zack about the last dream she'd had.

Glancing at Zack often on the ride to Santa Rosa on Friday morning, Melanie wondered what he was thinking, if he was sorry he'd asked her along. She'd tried to start a conversation, but both of her attempts had been met with short answers. She didn't know him well enough to pry. She didn't know him well enough to tell him she understood about loss and grief. That could lead to questions she wasn't prepared to answer.

As they entered the outskirts of Santa Rosa, Zack pointed out sections of the town as he drove. She saw a few apartment complexes but she was more attuned to the man beside her, more concerned about what was going on inside of him than thinking about another place to stay.

After winding through an up-scale development, he stopped in front of a two-story, stucco house with black wrought-iron trim. "This is it," he said with a finality that led Melanie to believe his feelings about it weren't final at all.

"Do you want me to wait here?" she asked as his hand went to the door.

"No, I'm just going to do a final check to make sure everything's the way I left it. I haven't been inside for the past few weeks."

Melanie met him on the flagstone path, and they walked up to the massive oak door. Zack pulled a key from his pocket, inserted it in the doorknob, and they stepped inside.

At once she saw that the house wasn't completely bare. Draperies still adorned the windows, and area rugs covered the hardwood floors.

"The new owners might want to clear out the curtains and the rugs, but I have no use for them, either," Zack remarked as he stepped deeper into the living room.

Melanie could tell the draperies were custom-made, the rugs of fine quality. She ventured a question. "How long did you live here?"

"Six years. Sherry and I bought the place right after we were married." After another cursory look around the room, he headed for the stairs.

Zack went up the steps first. Upstairs, Melanie wandered from room to room with him. This was a beautiful house with window seats, casement windows and an old-world feel to it. But it was empty now, and she knew Zack felt the emptiness more keenly than she did.

When they returned downstairs, she wandered into the kitchen and saw that it was high-tech. Zack found her examining the smooth-top stove. In a low voice he said, "Sherry didn't cook much, but she liked having the latest gadgets."

Slowly he crossed to the back door and opened it, staring outside for a few very long minutes. Melanie could see the tension in his shoulders, the stiffness of his neck, the rigidity of his posture. After that long look outside, he quickly went through the rest of the downstairs, even more remote than before.

Finally they stood in the foyer again, and she couldn't help but say, "I'm sure you miss it."

He turned to her then. "I don't miss it. I don't think about it. Just as I try not to think about Sherry's accident."

Instead of trying to find out more about the accident, she wanted to help him get through the pain. "You can't deny the grief you feel. It will just take that much longer to let up if you do."

From the first moment she'd met Zachary Morgan, she'd decided he was a kind man, a gentle man, but now there was no kindness or gentleness in his tone or his turbulent brown eyes. "I hired you as an interior decorator, not a counselor. Don't try to psychoanalyze me, Melanie."

He didn't have to add the words "bringing you along today was a mistake" but she could feel them and hear them as if he'd said them.

She hadn't even known him long enough for him to hurt her, but she did hurt at his words because she wanted to help him so much. She wanted to get to know him better. She wanted to solve the mystery behind her dreams.

She went out to the car to wait until he was finished saying goodbye to a house that had been part of his life.

Melanie's drive home with Zack was silent and, although he was in and out of the penthouse the rest of the day, she stayed in her room working on cost estimates. In some way she felt as if she belonged here with him and Amy, but in others she felt like an outsider.

At supper Melanie listened to Flo talk about her plans for the next day with her sister. They were going to leave early and drive to Reno. "We're leaving at 5:00 a.m., so I'm going to turn in the same time Amy does tonight. We'll probably get home about midnight tomorrow, hopefully with our pockets loaded and our wallets, too."

Silence fell over the kitchen, and Flo looked from Melanie to Zack and back to Melanie again, obviously aware of the tension between them. After she wiped her mouth with a napkin, she laid it on the table. "I think I'll give Amy her bath and get her ready for bed before I clean up everything in here. There are blueberry tarts in the fridge if you're interested."

When neither Zack nor Melanie showed any interest, Flo just arched her brows, lifted Amy from her high chair and went down the hall to the bathroom.

Zack stood, took his mug to the coffeepot, poured

coffee into it, then glanced at Melanie. "Would you like another cup?"

She held out her mug to him. "Half would be fine."

His fingertips brushed hers as he took it from her, their eyes met, and the world seemed to stand still—for one moment, for ten moments, for fifty moments. Melanie wasn't sure.

Then he set her mug on the counter and filled it halfway. When he returned to the table, he sat in Flo's chair, the one around the corner from Melanie and set her coffee in front of her. "I shouldn't have said what I did this morning."

He was wearing a denim shirt and black jeans. Melanie had never been so aware of the male aura he exuded. She put one hand around her mug then met his gaze. "I don't want to say the wrong thing."

He shook his head. "I don't want you to feel that way. You were right about this morning. It wasn't just a trip through a house I had to sell. It was a trip down memory lane, and it was much harder than I expected it to be."

"Memories are funny things," she said quietly. "You expect them to bring comfort, but instead they bring sadness and regret and wishes for stretches of time you know you'll never have again."

His gaze was probing. "You sound as if you know."

Careful, she told herself. *Be very careful.* She couldn't let her guard down entirely with Zack. Not yet. "Everyone has to cope with loss, and time does help. But even time doesn't make it easy. Losing my parents... Even after all these years, I miss them."

He brought his mug to his lips and took a few swallows. Amy's squeals of laughter from the bathroom floated down the hall to the kitchen. "Amy's kept me going," he admitted with a small smile. "She's that star I hooked the future onto, and I just let it pull me along. Everything I do now is for her."

Melanie could feel emotion brimming up in her eyes because she knew exactly what Zack meant. Kaitlyn had been her life, her hope, her promise of tomorrow. "You're very fortunate," she murmured.

"Yes, I am." The quiet between them seemed intimate, filled with understanding, and it was a bit unsettling.

Pushing away from the table and standing, Melanie began collecting the plates.

He stilled her hand. "You don't have to do that." His skin on hers was warm, taut, rougher than hers.

"I know Flo wants to turn in early," she managed.

"Do you have plans tomorrow?" he asked, releasing her and standing, too.

"Nothing specific. Why?"

"There's this party I have to go to tomorrow evening. The couple giving it are from near Clear Lake. They have a ranch up there. They want to introduce me to businessmen who will help this area grow. That type of thing is always more enjoyable if there's someone to talk to besides the other guests."

"What about Amy? Flo said she'd be gone till late."

"I already made arrangements with my dad to come over and stay with her. He's good with her, and he doesn't see her as often as he'd like."

"Is this a dress-up party?" She found herself wanting to get dressed up...for Zack.

"Sure is. Cecile said she won't let me in without a tie. I think you'll like Cecile and Don. They could probably throw some business your way once you finish my project."

"Uh-oh. That means I have to make a good impression."

"I don't think that will be a problem."

They were standing very close together. Zack's beard shadow was dark, and the urge to touch it made the tips of her fingers tingle. She didn't know if he was asking her to the party because he wanted to get to know her better or if he simply wanted company. It didn't matter. She'd take the opportunity to get to know *him* better.

"A party sounds nice."

Zack leaned a bit closer to her. She lifted her chin just an iota. The space between them diminished, but then Flo called from the bathroom. "Anyone want to say good-night to this little angel?"

Zack stepped back, Melanie took a deep breath, and he crossed the kitchen and walked down the hall to his daughter.

Melanie's sleeveless navy sheath could be casual when worn by itself. Tonight she'd added the bolero jacket with intricate piping, pearl drop earrings, and navy high heels. She knew she'd taken too much care fixing her hair and applying lipstick. She wanted to look good tonight. She wanted Zack to be proud of having her there with him.

A little voice inside her head said, *That sounds more like a wife's concern.*

Maybe so, maybe not. She just knew she was happy to be going out with Zack.

When the doorbell rang, she put the cap on her lipstick, eager to meet Zack's father. She came out of her room the same time Zack came out of Amy's. The little girl was dressed in her pajamas and she reached her arms out to Melanie. "Cawwy."

"Melanie's all prettied up," Zack told his daughter. "She might not want you tugging on her hair or putting wrinkles in her dress." Zack was talking to his daughter, but his gaze made a slow pass over Melanie with male appreciation that she found exciting.

With Amy's little arms outstretched, Melanie couldn't resist. She reached for her and gathered her into her arms. "This dress is practically wrinkle-free, and the wind will do more damage than Amy can do to my hair."

At that, Amy patted the hair just behind Melanie's ear and gave her a wide smile.

Zack chuckled. "I think she understands a lot more than we give her credit for."

When Melanie gazed into Amy's dark brown eyes, she sensed an innocent knowledge in the toddler. Again Melanie wondered if Amy sensed her mother's spirit and felt the connection that had brought her here.

Melanie glanced up at Zack and found him watching her carefully with an expression that was very sad. Melanie guessed it had something to do with missing his wife.

A moment later Zack turned and crossed to the door.

After walking into the living room with Amy, Melanie found Zack's father tossing his jacket over a chair.

"Melanie, this is Ted Morgan, my father," Zack said, making the introduction. "Pop, this is Melanie Carlotti. She's the interior decorator I told you about."

Ted Morgan was a few inches shorter than his son, with hair as dark brown as Zack's and almost as thick, though Ted's was liberally laced with gray. He was wearing a faded-plaid sport shirt and worn jeans and seemed a bit ill at ease as he extended his hand to her. "It's nice to meet you, Miss Carlotti. It is Miss?"

Swaying Amy with the natural rhythm of a mother, she smiled at him. "I use Ms."

"I see. One of those liberated women. I guess you're all that way now," he said with a sigh.

"Don't start, Pop," Zack warned.

Ted shot his son an exasperated look that told Melanie they'd had this discussion before.

"My son thinks I'm a throwback to the dark ages." There was a twinkle in his eye when he said it, but Melanie could sense a tension between Zack and his father.

With a wave of his hand that dismissed the whole discussion, Ted came over to his granddaughter and held his arms out to her. "Ready to have some real fun tonight, pumpkin?"

"She's still a little young for poker, Pop."

"Oh, but we'll start counting all her toes. That'll get her ready. Another year and I bet she'll be matching numbers on the cards."

Melanie laughed. She liked Zack's dad. He was warm and friendly and said what he thought. She could also see that Amy adored him. She was slapping her little hands against his.

"Uh-oh. Looks like she wants to play patty-cake. When you folks come home, I'll probably be all tuckered out and asleep on the couch."

Zack asked Melanie, "Ready to go?"

"Sure am."

To his dad he said, "The number for Cecile and Don Baker is on the refrigerator, and you have my cell number."

"Don't you worry about us. If we need anything, my car's got plenty of gas. I stopped in Cool Ridge for it. You really are out in the middle of nowhere up here."

"Not for long," Zack responded with an expression that told Melanie he and his dad had had this discussion before also.

Leaning toward his daughter, Zack kissed Amy. Melanie gave her a wave and they were out in the hall in the elevator and on their way.

On the drive Zack kept his eyes on the road…at least he tried to. Melanie was a definite distraction. So many things about her tugged at him, and he felt unsettled whenever he was around her. Amy was comfortable with her, as if Melanie had been taking care of her since she was born. And Melanie seemed to really enjoy Amy. Sherry had loved their daughter, but she hadn't always enjoyed her. Her career had been so damn important to her. She'd taken a leave to have Amy, but she couldn't wait to get back to her executive position at the cosmetics company. When she'd found out she was unexpectedly pregnant again, Amy had only been four months old, and Sherry hadn't wanted a new baby. Two to care for. Two in diapers. She'd shouted at him that she'd wanted her life back. It had been the worst argument they'd ever had and the reason he felt responsible for her accident. He couldn't help but wonder for the umpteenth time if she'd been intentionally trying to lose their baby…if she'd been driving to his trailer on the construction site to tell him she was going to terminate her pregnancy whether he wanted her to or not.

"The sky up here is so beautiful at night," Melanie murmured, breaking into his thoughts.

Relieved to take a respite from the guilt he carried, he glanced up, saw the three-quarter moon, the hundred twinkles of bright light. "Guess you couldn't see through the smog in L.A."

"Something like that."

"I probably don't appreciate this enough. It takes someone like you to remind me to take a good look at it again." At that he glanced over at her. His gut clenched and his blood raced faster. She was so blasted pretty, so blasted natural, such a blasted temptation.

He pressed his foot down on the accelerator a little harder, concluding tonight had been one of the worst ideas he'd ever had.

Chapter Four

A floodlight illuminated the front door of the Bakers' cedar-sided, rambling ranch house. There were also lights glowing on the outbuildings. Melanie caught a glimpse of a large stable, guest house and other utility buildings, then sneaked a sideways glance at Zack. He'd been silent toward the end of the drive, and she wasn't sure what to make of his sudden remoteness. Was he, too, trying to understand the vibrations between them?

His attitude became more casual again as a maid welcomed them inside and he introduced Melanie to Cecile and Don Baker. Cecile was a pretty brunette in her forties, and Don looked to be about the same age, though his hair was silver. They shook Melanie's hand enthusiastically.

"I hear you're doing a marvelous job decorating Zack's new offices," Cecile remarked. "I've been thinking about redoing our living room and dining room."

Don gave a loud groan.

His wife ignored him. "I'd love to have your ideas for something really different."

Her husband arched his brows. "She gets paid for her opinions, honey."

Melanie laughed. "I'd be glad to give you some ideas. I'll get a feel for the rooms while we mingle."

Shaking his head, Don said, "I can see my nice comfortable life is going to get disturbed."

"It doesn't have to, unless you make major renovations," Melanie offered with a smile.

"Then please, don't put major renovations into any of your suggestions."

Cecile gave her husband a playful punch in the arm, then she turned her attention again to Zack. "I just wanted to give you fair warning. Tom Kellison is here, a reporter from the *Santa Rosa Gazette*. He's doing photos and a layout of the new stable for the Weekend Style section. He asked me who was coming tonight and I mentioned your name. I think he's interested in doing a piece on your new headquarters and what that will mean to the expansion of the area. I told him I'd introduce you, but you might run into him on your own."

Melanie could see there were almost thirty people milling about, sitting on the long sofas and love seats in the living room, chatting in the dining room. She suspected there were more guests outside.

"No problem," Zack assured Cecile. "I'll be glad to talk to him. It's good publicity for the stores."

Cecile nodded to the bar, set up along one corner of the living room. "Go get yourself something to drink and eat and have fun."

The doorbell was ringing again, so Zack and Melanie

moved into the living room. Zack's hand was at her elbow as he guided her toward the bar, and she could feel the zing of his touch all the way to her toes.

"What would you like to drink?" he asked.

"A glass of Bianca would be good."

"Bianca it is."

As Melanie and Zack got caught up in conversations with people Zack knew and others who just joined in, she took special note of the living room and dining room area, already planning what Cecile could do with it. As more and more guests entered the two rooms, the temperature became warmer. She was about to remove her jacket when Zack asked, "Would you like to see the stables? It's probably cooler outside."

"Surc. I've never been around horses much, but I've always wanted the chance to learn to ride. Do you ride?"

"Now and then. I brought Amy out here a couple of months ago with Flo. I rode while they just looked at the horses. It's hard to find the time, even though I have an open-ended invitation from Cecile and Don."

"And when you have free time, you'd rather spend it with Amy."

"Exactly."

She and Zack seemed to connect on so many levels, and she saw the sparks of realization in his eyes that said he noticed it, too.

They walked toward the outbuildings on a paved path that was kind to Melanie's high heels. Out in the open, with the cool night air brushing against them, the sky seemed even blacker, the points of light even brighter, and the glow of the moon even more magical. A few guests exited the stables as they neared the doors. Zack opened the large door for Melanie and waited as she preceded him inside. Her shoulder brushed his arm as the rustling of hay and the smell of horses and saddle leather wrapped around them.

There was a man standing at one of the horse stalls feeding a gray mare a few carrot sticks from the veggie platter. He smiled at them as they came down the walkway. Then, cocking his head, he asked, "Aren't you Zack Morgan?"

"Yes, I am."

The man extended his hand. "Tom Kellison. Cecile told me you'd be coming."

The men shook hands, and then Tom's gaze fell on Melanie. Zack explained, "This is Melanie Carlotti. She's doing the interior design work on my headquarters."

"Carlotti," Tom mused. "That name sounds familiar. Are you from this area?"

"No. From Los Angeles." Her heart pounded so loudly she wondered if the reporter could hear it.

"So was I until a few months ago when I moved up here to take the position at the *Gazette*."

"I'm sure you meet a lot of people in your profession, many whose names sound alike."

His eyes were questioning as they found hers again. "Maybe so. I'm either blessed or cursed with the talent of never forgetting a name. I'm sure it'll come to me. Most things do."

A wave of fear swept through Melanie. The story about the fire had been in the L.A. papers. Thank goodness she wouldn't be seeing Tom Kellison again to remind him of where he'd heard her name. She just hoped he didn't remember by the end of the evening.

Turning his attention again to Zack, Tom asked, "Is it all right if I give you a call to set up some time for an interview? I'm doing a fairly extensive article on the economics of the area.''

Immediately Zack took a business card from his inside pocket. ''This is my home number. I'm on the road a lot these days until the headquarters are finished. If you leave a message there, I'll be sure to get it and I'll get back to you.''

Tom nodded and smiled. ''I understand.'' The reporter motioned around the stables. ''Enjoy your tour. It's some setup. It was a pleasure meeting you.'' With a final wave he exited the stable and headed toward the house.

''Carlotti isn't a usual name,'' Zack commented. ''I wonder why he thinks he remembers it.''

Not wanting to dwell on the subject, Melanie moved toward a pinto pony. ''Isn't he pretty?''

Zack laughed. ''I'm not sure Cecile and Don describe their horses in terms of *pretty*.''

The overhead light created a subtle intimacy that Melanie was well aware of in the shadowed barn. She could feel Zack's gaze on her as he went on, ''That's a term to describe a woman, one who looks like you do tonight.''

His gaze heated her, and she couldn't ignore it. She couldn't ignore him or the pull toward him that she was becoming accustomed to. Raising her head, she looked up at him. ''Thank you.''

They were standing very close, and the only sound was the slight swishing of a horse's tail. Zack's brown gaze seemed to swallow her, and her breathing was coming so fast she thought it might stop altogether. She stood perfectly still as his hand came to her face. She'd longed for his touch from the day she'd met him. Now it was gentle as his thumb brushed her cheekbone and then glided into her hair. But when he ruffled the hair at her temple, he suddenly stilled and she realized why.

"That's a scar," he said, gently tracing his finger over it. "What happened?"

She could tell him why she'd come to him, why she'd sought him out, but she knew her feelings for him were growing deeper. More than anything, she didn't want him to send her away. He'd do that if she told him about the dreams. He'd think she was crazy.

"When you asked about the two years I didn't work... I was in an accident. It's still too painful to talk about. It took me a long time to recover."

After he studied her for a lengthy moment, he said, "I don't like talking or thinking about the past, either." His hand moved from her face to the nape of her neck. He murmured, "Maybe we can forget about it altogether." And then his lips came down on hers.

There was nothing tentative or experimental about the kiss. From the moment Zack's lips met hers, there was intense heat, potent desire and yearning hunger on both their parts. When his tongue swept along her bottom lip, she opened to him willingly. Her hands went to his shoulders, and she could feel his strength, the restrained tension in his body. He took the kiss deeper, and she knew she'd never been kissed like this before, never felt the fiery excitement running through her, never dreamed a kiss could be this sensual or yearning or perfect.

Then Zack abruptly released her, and all the sensations stopped so suddenly, she felt dizzy.

He looked troubled as he said gruffly, "That was a mistake."

A mistake because there was so much feeling between them already? So much desire? "Why was it a mistake?'' she asked, needing to know...because she was falling in love with him.

"Because you're working for me. You're staying under my roof, and I won't take advantage of either of those."

"You didn't take advantage of me, Zack."

He looked surprised for a moment, then a guardedness was back in his eyes. "Maybe not, but I don't need my life any more complicated than it is. I imagine you don't, either."

She wanted to tell Zack that love shouldn't complicate his life, it should enrich it. But she suspected he didn't want to hear that. He certainly wouldn't believe that she was falling in love with him after just one week. So she kept silent, and he took that as agreement.

"We'd better get back to the party," he said gruffly. "There are other guests up there I want to talk to before we leave." Then he turned away from her and walked to the stable door, waiting for her to join him.

This time as they walked the path to the house, it was as if a wall divided them. Melanie knew she'd have to be careful or she'd be out of Zack's life before she even had a chance to decorate his offices.

The drive back to Zack's penthouse was rife with tension...all kinds of tension. The knowledge they would be sleeping under the same roof didn't help. Melanie had had a taste of whatever was sparking between them, and it would be much harder to put it out of her head. Would Zack have the same problem? Maybe the kiss hadn't meant anything to him. Maybe the chemistry was something he could ignore.

When Zack unlocked the door to the penthouse, Melanie went inside and saw Ted Morgan stretched out on the sofa. He was watching TV, though, not sleeping.

"If you want to stay the night instead of driving back, Pop, that pulls out into a bed," Zack suggested.

"Nah. I'm going to drive back. My old bones like my own bed. Amy's been sleeping soundly since nine-thirty. I checked on her a couple of times."

"Sometimes she wakes up around midnight. I'll make sure she's still asleep."

Sliding his legs over the side of the sofa, Ted sat up. "Good party?" he asked Melanie.

"It was very nice."

After Zack left the room to check on Amy, Ted said in a low voice, "My son likes you."

She wasn't sure what to say to that. "I like Zack. He's a great employer—"

"I don't mean that work stuff. When he looks at you, I see sparks in his eyes. I haven't seen them since he first met Sherry."

"Mr. Morgan..."

"Quit the Mr. Morgan stuff. It's Ted. And you don't have to be embarrassed. It would do Zack good to get interested in a woman again. The only thing is—" Ted cleared his throat "—Zack's never been a one-night-here or one-night-there kind of man, if you know what I mean."

"I know what you mean."

"He said you're from L.A. Are you planning on staying around here?"

"I'm considering it, but...we really are just working together."

"You never know what could develop," Ted concluded with a gleam in his eye.

After that kiss and the way Zack had backed away,

Melanie had a feeling he wasn't going to let anything further develop. That thought filled her with such sadness she wanted to cry.

After Sunday lunch Melanie was helping Flo clean off the table. Zack had taken Amy into her room to change her. He'd been casually polite this morning, sending off plenty of signals that told Melanie he had no intention of discussing what had happened last night in the stable or that he put much store in it. She wondered if he simply wasn't ready to get involved again or if he was still so in love with his wife he couldn't bear the thought of having a relationship with another woman. She understood both reasons. She just wished...

Flo suddenly put down the platter, yawned widely and covered her mouth with her hand. "I'm too old for these long days and late nights. It was fun coming back with a pocketbook full of quarters, but I'm going to pay for it all day. I was planning on going into Cool Ridge and getting groceries this afternoon, but I might fall asleep at the wheel."

"If you make me a list, I'll drive in to get whatever you need," Melanie offered.

Zack came into the kitchen just then carrying Amy. "What do you need?" he asked Flo.

"Groceries for the week, diapers and countless other things if I put my mind to thinking about it."

"Reno a little too rough for you?" Zack asked, amused.

Flo made a face at him. "Your day will come," she muttered.

They all laughed.

"I offered to go into Cool Ridge for her," Melanie explained.

"Why don't we both go and take Amy with us? That way Flo will have the place to herself and can really rest."

Surprised, Melanie glanced at Zack. After last night, she suspected he wouldn't want to be alone with her. Yet handling groceries as well as a child could be tricky, and they wouldn't really be alone. Amy would be an active little chaperone.

"If Amy's along, the list will probably double," Flo said in a mock whisper to Melanie. "Her father has a knack for picking up everything she wants."

Zack smiled. "You know what they say about daddy's little girl." His gaze met Melanie's, and she remembered the conversation they'd had about that. She also remembered the touch of Zack's hand on her face, the texture of his lips on hers, the feel of his taut shoulder muscles.

She quickly picked up the vegetable bowl on the table and took it to the counter, hoping Zack didn't see the remembrance of all of it in her eyes.

A half hour later, Amy babbled and pointed during the drive to town, and conversation didn't seem necessary. Cool Ridge had a supermarket that—from the looks of it—had everything they might need.

Zack pointed to the back of the parking lot. "In the spring they're going to enlarge to get ready for the boom of development. Cool Ridge might find itself growing faster than it wants to."

"That would be a shame," Melanie said, meaning it.

The sliding glass doors to the store opened as they walked toward them. "Do you like small towns?"

"I've never really lived in one. But I like the quiet out here. I like feeling less rushed."

Securing a cart, Zack settled Amy in the child's seat and strapped her in with the safety belt. As they went inside, she pointed to the bananas in the produce department. "'Nanas," she said firmly.

"She's going to be talking a mile a minute before you know it," Melanie remarked, thinking about Kaitlyn's vocabulary at the same age.

Zack ruffled his daughter's hair and picked up a bunch of bananas. "I can't wait. It'll beat trying to guess what she wants."

Just then a couple with three children around the ages of three, five and seven came bounding into the store. The children were chattering, the husband and wife were talking to each other as they strolled down the aisle. They made a picture that squeezed Melanie's heart.

Her turmoil must have been reflected on her face because Zack asked, "What's wrong?"

She hadn't realized she'd been staring. "Nothing's wrong," she said with a shake of her head. "I'd just like to have a brood of kids like that someday." To her dismay she couldn't keep tears from welling up in her eyes as she remembered Kaitlyn and dreams and a future that would never be.

Seeing her emotion, Zack didn't seem disturbed by it. "I wanted several children, too, but that won't happen now."

"Because your wife died?"

"It was a dream I had with her, and the dream's gone."

"Don't you believe in having new dreams?" Melanie asked softly.

Zack shook his head. "Dreams are like bubbles. They burst, leaving lots of disappointment and heartache. It's better not to have them."

That wasn't a concept Melanie could accept. "Don't you have dreams for Amy?"

"That's different. I have goals for Amy, not dreams. Goals are something you can work toward and achieve. They're substantial and won't slip through your fingers like sand."

There was pain in his voice and in his eyes and she couldn't dispute what he was saying. However, since her transplants, she'd come to a whole new understanding of dreams. She couldn't share that with him, though. At least, not yet.

Amy wiggled in the cart. "Go, go, go," she insisted. Her childish command broke the intimacy of the moment and the seriousness of their discussion.

"Okay, we'll go," Zack soothed her and guided the cart down the aisle away from any more sharing that might tell Melanie what he was all about—about his vulnerabilities, about what he was feeling inside.

When they stopped beside a display of apple juice, Melanie asked Zack about something that had been on her mind. "Did you look over the pictures of the sculptures I gave you?"

As he set the bottle of juice in the cart, he glanced over his shoulder at her. "By that artist in San Francisco?"

"Yes. The pictures are good, but I really think you ought to see his work in person. There are other pieces for sale besides the ones on the flier. If the piece is going to sit in your lobby, it will be the first thing anyone sees when they come inside. It will be an important statement, sort of like a preliminary image of you and how you work and what you're all about.''

''Uh-oh. Choosing a sculpture sounds awfully complicated. I just thought I'd pick out something I'd like to look at.''

Melanie laughed. ''I guess I'm seeing it from an interior decorator's standpoint.''

''That's what I'm paying you to do.''

She had the feeling he'd said that to put up a barrier between them again. He was the employer and she was the employee. That was the extent of it.

So be it. He still had to choose a sculpture. ''I checked on Vincente's hours, and he's in on Saturday from eleven to three. If you don't have time or don't want to make the trip, I suppose I could take a camera and shoot photographs.''

Zack's gaze seemed to pass over every feature of her face. She felt it almost as strongly as if he'd touched her. He finally said, ''I'll check my schedule and see if I'm free.''

''I like that one.''

The certainty in Zack's voice didn't surprise Melanie as they stood in Vincente Largo's studio, examining each sculpture. The one Zack was admiring was distinctly Largo. It was a bronze representation of a mountain with one man perched on top, another man at the bottom. Four feet high, the piece had a majesty about it that captured the onlooker. Instead of the usual pedestal, the mountain perched atop a granite base that seemed made for it, wide and jagged, a continuation of the work of art.

''It's expensive,'' she noted.

''I'm only doing this once.''

Already she knew that Zack was a man who wanted to get things right the first time, and he put everything he had into doing that.

He glanced down at her. "You were right, I needed to see these. Pictures wouldn't have done them justice." He nodded outside to the dock. "Do you want to get something to eat before we go back? There's a good restaurant not far from here. They serve a great swordfish salad. I'm sure Dad won't mind spending a little more time with Amy." It was Flo's day off and Ted had jumped at the chance to spend the day with his granddaughter.

"Do you come to San Francisco often?" she asked, curious about everything concerning him.

"One of my stores is here."

He turned toward the back room where Vincente had disappeared shortly after they'd arrived. "Let's make arrangements to have this delivered. The grand opening is the first week in January, so why don't we say around mid-December. Everything should almost be finished by then."

"If it's not, we'll both be tearing our hair out."

He studied her for a few moments. "Have you ever worn your hair long?"

"Don't you like it short?" she asked with a teasing smile.

"It's great short. But you just seem like a woman who would like longer hair."

This man was entirely too perceptive. "I wore it long, before the f—" She was about to say fire, but instead she amended, "Before the accident."

"Sorry," he said. "I didn't mean to bring up bad memories."

"That's okay." She blocked as many of those memories as she could.

Apparently Zack could see the shadows of them in her eyes because he stepped closer. "Sometime you'll have to tell me about it."

"Sometime," she murmured.

Their walk along Fisherman's Wharf was companionable yet tinged with a tension that always hung between them. She'd worn a hunter-green sweater and slacks today while Zack's casual black slacks and red, long-sleeved Henley shirt marked him as a striking figure as they strolled along the wood piers, past shops and restaurants, breathing the salty air. A magician performed tricks as a crowd gathered around him. A unique-looking antique shop beckoned to Melanie. When Zack noticed her interest, they went inside and she pointed out a few pieces she'd like to own someday.

After they exited the shop, Zack pointed to a café farther along the pier. As he put his hand in the small of her back to guide her inside, she realized how much she enjoyed being with him...how she felt complete when she was beside him.

Over lunch they enjoyed the view of the water and talked about Zack's headquarters, the grand opening and other places they'd seen and traveled to in their lifetimes. Melanie explained how she'd taken a trip in college to the Grand Canyon, how she'd hiked until she had blisters all over the bottoms of her feet and had to soak them for a week after she got home.

"Pop used to take us on road trips," Zack told her.

"Where did you go?" She was hoping he'd tell her more.

"When my mother was alive, we took a trip to Yellowstone. After she died, Pop dragged me back there one summer. It wasn't the same.''

"When did you lose her?" Melanie asked.

"When I was eleven."

Zack saw the waiter then and motioned to him for the check. After he inserted bills into the folder the waiter had given him, he stood and gestured to the side of the restaurant. "Let's go out this way. I want to show you something."

The side door to the restaurant led to a terrace and a small enclosed garden perched over the water. Brilliant pink and purple petunias as well as white and red geraniums bloomed in pots everywhere. Latticework above the garden held wisteria vines.

"It's so pretty!" She turned in a circle, looking all around her.

"I didn't want you to leave without seeing it. And I think I needed to see it again, too."

"Why?" she asked, facing Zack.

"The last time Sherry and I were here— It's the last time I remember us being truly happy."

His words triggered a reaction in Melanie, and she blurted out, "That's not true."

At her outburst, she froze. She knew the words and the feelings that went with them weren't her own. They belonged to Sherry Morgan!

Chapter Five

Zack studied Melanie curiously. She'd sounded so vehement. It was nice she was trying to reassure him, but he remembered the changes in his marriage all too well.

Melanie's cheeks were flushed. "I mean...you remember that moment as a happy one, but I'm sure there were lots of others after that."

He shook his head. "Once we had Amy, everything changed. Sherry really didn't like being home and cooped up with a baby. Or maybe she had postpartum depression. I just know our relationship shifted from the moment she found out she was pregnant." Her second pregnancy had brought a division between them that might have torn their marriage apart.

The breeze blew Melanie's hair across her cheek and she brushed it away. "Having a baby can turn a woman's world upside down. That little life inside of her depends on her for absolutely everything from the moment of conception. That's a tremendous bond, and it changes everything about her world."

"It does that to a man, too."

"I guess it does. But I think men look at a child as more of a responsibility. For a woman I don't know if the umbilical cord is ever really cut."

"You seem to know a lot about it."

He watched as she took a deep breath. "I just know that being a parent has to be an awesome responsibility." Then she averted her gaze and murmured, "Maybe we'd better start back."

With Melanie, Zack almost felt the freedom to confide everything inside his head, as if she could help him sort it. Now as he gazed down at her, the garden felt like an intimate hideaway where they were the only two people in San Francisco. When he reached out to nudge her face to him again, he knew she felt the chemistry between them as strongly as he did because she trembled.

There was a wisdom in Melanie that he found intriguing. He found everything about her intriguing, and he couldn't forget how she'd felt in his arms. The memory was so alive, had tempted him so many hours of his day. No matter how many times he told himself he should stay away from her, he found himself creating situations to *be* with her. Now her blue eyes were filled with emotion that seemed to draw him in. Though he knew he was being reckless, right now he didn't care. He needed that rush of desire to remind him he was still alive, to remind him he was in his prime, to remind him there was more to life than work and Amy.

Resisting the urge to kiss Melanie didn't seem important anymore as he curved his arm around her, brought her close, and bent his head to her. She was sweetness and brightness and caring. He longed for all of those. Her mouth opened under his like a gift she was giving them both. Their first kiss had been explosive. This one was filled with longing and need and hunger that neither of them understood. He found himself imagining them in bed together—

What was he doing? A few minutes ago his mind had been filled with thoughts of his marriage to Sherry. What kind of man was he? Physical needs had driven him in his youth, but certainly not now. Yet he felt as primed as a teenager again when he was around Melanie, and he almost resented the effect she had on him. He wasn't ready to jump into an involvement with a woman...not any woman...not until the pain from the accident, as well as the guilt, faded. All of it was still too much with him.

Willing his pulse to slow and his blood to cool, he stepped away from her. "We really should be getting back. I think Pop has plans tonight."

Melanie's face was flushed and she'd never looked prettier. But Zack ignored that fact and crossed to the archway that led to a path around the restaurant. It was time for him to get back to reality. Time to get back home.

Ted Morgan's ranch-style house with its tan siding and brown trim was the same size and shape as most of the other houses on his street. Melanie had only caught a quick glimpse of the inside when they'd dropped off Amy earlier. Now as Ted opened the door for them, he was smiling broadly. "Is San Francisco still in one piece?"

When Zack didn't respond, Melanie did. "It's still as beautiful as always."

"With or without fog," Ted Morgan agreed. "Amy's napping. Do you want me to get her up?"

Zack shook his head and started down the hall to one of the bedrooms. "No, I'll do it."

Ted studied his son's back as he walked away and gave a deep sigh. Then he motioned to the brown-and-gold-tweed sofa. "Have a seat. Can I get you something to drink?"

"I think Zack wants to get back." It had been so difficult not being completely honest with Zack in the garden of the restaurant. But the stakes were greater now. Although she might have felt Sherry's feelings for a few moments, she knew 99 percent of the other feelings had nothing to do with Sherry. She was falling in love with Zack Morgan and there was nothing she could do about it.

"He could stay awhile and visit," Ted muttered.

"Don't you have plans tonight?"

Zack's father shrugged. "Just a card party at the senior center. Nothing I can't skip. I would if Zack actually wanted to spend some time here with me."

Not sure exactly what to say, she reassured him. "I'm sure he does want to spend time with you. But with work and Amy…"

"Nope, it's always been this way. Ever since his mom died."

Suspecting Ted needed to tell someone about this, Melanie waited.

"Jane had cancer," he explained. "The doctors told me she only had a matter of weeks. I didn't tell Zack she was going to die. When he was at school one day, I had to take her to the hospital. She never came home again. Zack didn't have a chance to say goodbye, and he's always hated me for that."

"Have you ever talked to him about it?"

"We don't talk much, never have, probably never

will. I hoped when he had a family of his own… But things between us seem to have gotten worse since Sherry died.''

Because Zack hadn't had a chance to say goodbye to his wife, either? Melanie wondered.

Amy's chirping little voice ended the conversation as Zack carried his daughter down the hall and into the living room. "I'm not sure she ever went to sleep," Zack said to his dad. "She was talking to BoBo when I went in."

"She was only down about half an hour. Maybe she'll nap for you on the ride home. The car always put *you* to sleep. When you were two months old, you had colic so bad your mom and I would take a drive at midnight just to get some peace and quiet.''

Seeming to ignore his dad's comment, Zack picked up Amy's diaper bag. "I'll bring diapers next time Amy stays here. You're almost out."

"Don't worry about it. I'll pick some up at the store.''

"You don't have to spend your pension on things like that. I'll take care of it."

Ted's mouth formed a taut line. "Fine."

The underlying tension Melanie had sensed between Zack and his dad was acutely apparent today. Was Zack really still angry at his dad after all these years?

On the drive back to Cool Ridge she decided to ask him. Amy had fallen asleep in her car seat. Dusk was settling in, and Zack's headlights automatically went on as the light faded. The silence between them reverberated with so many things—the conversation they'd had in the garden behind the restaurant, the need that had risen in their kiss, Zack's distance afterward. He didn't want to be attracted to her, that was obvious. Though reason told her she was an outsider to Zack's family situation, something strong inside of her was urging her to discuss it with him.

Sherry?

Melanie wasn't sure about that this time. Maybe her feelings for Zack were just growing so deep she wanted to help him come to terms with whatever was wrong between him and his dad.

She plunged in. "Your father told me your mom died of cancer."

Zack gave her a long sideways glance. "Did you two have a heart-to-heart?"

"Not exactly. I think he was upset that—"

"Upset about what?" Zack asked curiously.

"Upset that you don't want to spend more time with him."

"Pop and I rub each other the wrong way."

"Is that because he didn't tell you your mom was dying and she went to the hospital and never came home again?"

Zack's hands on the wheel tightened, his jaw set, and then he slanted her a glance that was sharp. "I don't understand why he told you any of this when you're not even a member of the family."

Stung, Melanie turned away and gazed unseeingly out the side window. That's what she got for trying to become involved in Zack's life. Though she shouldn't be, she felt unreasonably hurt because Zack's words told her he still considered her a stranger. Just because they'd shared a couple of kisses didn't mean they were even friends.

They drove the rest of the way in silence.

Unsettled by his day with Melanie, Zack had hoped to escape to his office when they returned to the penthouse. But Flo had prepared a light supper even though it was her day off.

She informed him, "I have to eat, too."

Regretting what he'd said to Melanie, Zack tried to engage her in conversation throughout supper. Everything about her made him feel turned inside out. She was so different from Sherry. She liked antiques and tradition and old-fashioned flowers like petunias. Sherry had liked contemporary furniture, exotic orchids and never liked to do the same thing twice.

As he'd kissed Melanie, he'd felt as if he was betraying Sherry in some way. It didn't make sense. But that was the way he felt. Then Melanie had tried to become an advocate for his dad...

Did his dad really want to spend more time with him? They'd always had separate lives. Maybe since his father had retired he had too much time on his hands.

"Oh, by the way," Flo said to Melanie. "You had a call. Jordan Wilson. He'd like you to call him this evening if you can. I told him I'd give you the message."

Watching Melanie's face, Zack saw her expression relax and her mouth turn up in a smile. Was this Wilson someone she was involved with?

"Thanks, Flo, I'll give him a call after dinner. Your chili's great by the way. Hot enough to make my tongue tingle but not too hot that I need to wash it down with glasses of water."

As Flo laughed, Zack thought about Melanie's tongue stroking his, the desire that had gripped him both times they'd kissed. He suddenly needed to get away from her and the turmoil she caused inside of him.

Pushing his chair back, he stood. "Supper was great,

Flo. Would you mind putting Amy to bed tonight? I need to spend a few hours in my office.''

"No problem. I brought the mail in this afternoon. It's on the table in the hall. Looks like mostly bills to me."

Melanie was sipping tea.

"Don't feel you have to get up early tomorrow," he told her. "I'm going to take Amy to a street fair in Santa Rosa."

When Melanie nodded, he thought about asking her to go along, then he decided against it. They'd crossed too many boundaries already and he needed time with his daughter on his own.

On his way to his office, he stopped at the table in the hall and saw the two stacks of mail. His was much larger than Melanie's. She had three letters—legal-size envelopes—and the top one caught his eye. Rather, the return address did. It was from a Collin Bates. But it was the title after the name that interested Zack. He was a private investigator.

Why was Melanie Carlotti receiving mail from a private investigator?

Logic told him he really knew very little about her.

It was better that way.

Zack and Amy had just gotten back from the street fair when Jordan arrived on Sunday. Melanie had returned his call, and he'd said he wanted to see how she was doing for himself by asking her to dinner. She'd accepted his invitation gratefully, needing his solid sense of purpose, needing his advice.

Now Melanie introduced the two men, explaining to Zack that she and Jordan were going to dinner. Zack and Jordan shook hands, though it was a short, perfunctory shake without much congeniality behind it. She didn't know what to make of Zack's scowl as he looked Jordan over from his brown hair and square jaw, to his designer polo shirt, casual slacks and Italian loafers.

"You drove up from L.A.?" Zack asked.

"Yes, I did. I've only been to Clear Lake once or twice. This is a nice area."

"A long way to come for dinner." Zack's tone was neutral.

"I'm staying the night in Cool Ridge and driving back in the morning. It seemed more sensible." He smiled at Melanie. "The same motel where you stayed your first night here. But I'm sure I'll have a different experience than you did. The manager told me he only had one other reservation for tonight. I'll have the place to myself."

Zack's scowl deepened. "So Melanie told you about what happened?"

"She sure did."

Melanie had just told Jordan about it last night when he'd asked her where he could stay in the area.

An awkward silence fell over the group and Jordan checked his watch. "I made reservations for seven. We should go." He nodded to Zack. "Nice to have met you."

As Melanie followed Jordan out of the penthouse, she noticed Zack was still frowning.

Once she and Jordan were inside the elevator, Jordan said to her, "He doesn't like me."

"Don't be ridiculous. Zack doesn't know you."

"I'm a man and I'm your friend and he doesn't like me. Trust me on this, Melanie. He's interested in you."

The elevator came to a halt. They exited, and instead

of going into the garage, went down the short hall to an outside door. Jordan held it for her and they left the building.

Once she was seated inside Jordan's Lexus, she stared up at the penthouse. "He doesn't want to be interested in me, Jordan."

"How do you know that?"

"He always backs off after..." Her voice trailed off.

"Just how involved are you?"

"We kissed. That's all."

He looked over at her with that brotherly expression she knew very well. "You need to tell him why you're here."

With a sigh she shook her head. "I can't do that. I'm beginning to feel so much for Zack, and if I tell him, he might banish me from his life entirely."

"This isn't about just finding answers anymore is it?" her friend asked knowingly.

"That's still a big part of it. But...no. I'm becoming so fond of Amy. Every time I look at her— I don't know if the longing I feel is because of Kaitlyn or if the feeling is Sherry Morgan's. And Zack...I'm more sure about those feelings. I know I feel drawn to Zack, and it has nothing to do with his wife. I can't explain it, Jordan. I just know that where Zack's concerned, I can separate my feelings from Sherry's."

As Jordan studied her, she felt her cheeks flush. "I really do sound like I should be telling this to a psychiatrist, don't I?"

"Anybody but you and I would think so, too."

Every day she was thankful for Jordan's support and Barbara's, too. Both had encouraged her to do whatever she had to to find peace of mind. "I paid the last installment on Collin Bates's bill. When I hired him, I never expected to be living with Zack, to feel so much for him and Amy…''

''Where do you see all of this headed?'' Jordan asked.

''I'm not sure. I just know that something is unfinished between Zack and Sherry. He won't be able to love again until it's settled.''

''And if it doesn't get settled, what happens to you?''

''I don't know. I just know this is something I have to see through.''

After he slipped the key in the ignition, he turned to look at her again. ''Well, I think you need a night to forget about all of it. We're going dining and dancing and we're going to catch up and escape. How does that sound?''

Her heart lifted and she gave him a smile. ''It sounds wonderful. Thanks for being my friend, Jordan, as well as my doctor.''

''Anytime. Now, let's go paint the town red.''

At 1:00 a.m. Melanie unlocked the penthouse door. She didn't know if she and Jordan had painted the town red, but she'd had a pleasant evening with him. They'd had a luscious supper at a fine restaurant near Clear Lake, danced a few sets and then gone back to his motel room to talk because the music was too loud at the restaurant. They'd had a lot to catch up on.

Before he'd left her at the door, he'd warned her gently, ''The holidays are coming.''

''I know.''

''Just be aware of it, Melanie. Don't try to deny the feelings that come up, or they'll just come back to bite you.'' Then he'd given her a warm hug.

When she let herself inside now, she saw Zack was

sitting in the living room, the TV turned down low as he watched a wilderness adventure show.

He came to his feet when he saw her and he didn't look happy. "Where the hell have you been?" His eyes raked over her as if he was expecting to figure out something.

"I went out to dinner."

"Dinner until 1:00 a.m.?"

Could that be jealousy she saw in his eyes? Did he care that she'd gone to dinner with Jordan? "We had dinner, danced a little and then it was too noisy to talk so we went back to the motel."

At that, Zack's brown eyes grew turbulent. "I bet that was cozy. Didn't you realize how late it was getting? That I might be worried something happened to you?"

So he'd been worried that she'd been abducted? Maybe he felt responsible for her because she was living under his roof. She didn't want him feeling responsible for her. She wanted...

Her deepening feelings for Zack scared her. What would happen when she told him who she really was? What would happen when she told him that some of her feelings might belong to his wife?

It was all so bizarre...including Zack's sense of righteous indignation now as he acted like a protective father. What had he said yesterday? *You're not even a member of the family.* That still hurt and he hadn't apologized for it, probably because he didn't think there was anything to apologize for.

She didn't owe him any explanations. "As you said yesterday, Zack, I'm not a member of your family. What I do in my off time is none of your business."

Suddenly everything seemed to overwhelm her—her

stay here, the trip to San Francisco, Zack's attitude toward her. With tears much too close to the surface, she headed for her room and didn't look back.

The hours passed quickly on Monday as Mclanie made sure all her measurements for windows were exact. She'd fill out the order forms for the blinds and the draperies later. Though she'd seen Zack several times during the day consulting with the workmen, he hadn't stopped to talk to her. The tension between them was as taut as it had been the night before and the night before that.

That evening Flo informed Melanie that Zack was leaving on a backpacking trip on Thursday. He and one of his store managers were outfitting a group of clients. The clients were prestigious enough in their own circles to bring more business to Zack's chain.

Melanie didn't even have a private conversation with Zack before he left on the trip.

While he was gone, she let herself relax more with Flo and Amy, not worried about his watchful eyes on her. She asked Flo if she could put Amy to bed Thursday night, and the housekeeper enjoyed the break. On Saturday Flo and Melanie took Amy to Cool Ridge to a park, but rain started falling and they had to come home early. It was still a nice day, though, and that evening they played with Amy on the floor, building with blocks and rolling a ball among them. They were putting Amy to bed when the phone rang. Flo went into the kitchen to answer it and came back a few minutes later.

"Was it Zack?" Melanie asked. She knew he had his cell phone with him.

"No, it was a friend of mine—Emma Fockelman.

She lives in Santa Rosa. She wants me to come to dinner tomorrow. But I told her Zack was away."

"I'm here. I'd be glad to watch Amy."

"I don't know…"

"If you're worried Zack might not approve, I understand. Why don't you give him a call and ask him? If he hesitates at all, don't worry about offending me. But I'd love taking care of her for a few hours."

Flo smiled. "I'll call him now."

From what Flo said after her call to Zack, he didn't have any reservations about letting Melanie care for Amy for a few hours. He should be back around dinner time.

"Then it's settled," Melanie said with a light feeling bubbling up inside her because she'd have Amy all to herself for a couple of hours.

Flo left around four on Sunday in a drizzling rain, and Melanie played with and cuddled and sang to Amy as if she'd been doing it forever. She baked chicken, mashed potatoes and boiled peas for supper, then opened a jar of applesauce for dessert—all foods Amy liked best. The rain had changed to hard driving sheets by the time she put Amy to bed. She hoped Flo and Zack would be careful driving.

By eight-thirty, she suspected the rain had delayed Zack. Settling on the sofa with a book she hadn't had time to finish, she slipped on her reading glasses and tried to concentrate on the page. But she couldn't help thinking about Zack. When the key turned in the door around nine-thirty, everything inside of her went on alert.

He came inside, carrying a duffel bag and backpack. He looked as if he'd been wrestling with a bear for the past week, and he was wet from head to toe.

"Zack, what happened?"

"Rain happened," he said with a grimace. "Two days of it. It was a great way to show our customers how well the equipment worked, but even rain gear can't keep you dry hiking in this."

"You don't have any rain gear on!"

"I left it in the garage." He started unlacing his boots. "I'd better leave these out here. I don't want to track up everything."

She laid her book and glasses on the coffee table. "Is there anything I can do to help?"

"I just want to get a hot shower and something to eat. Is Amy in bed?"

"A little while ago. But she was already half-asleep when I tucked her in." Melanie crossed to him. "Drop your clothes outside the bathroom door and I'll put them in the washing machine. I made chicken and mashed potatoes for supper. Would you like some warmed up?"

"That sounds terrific. We subsisted on backpacking rations. I'm ready for real food."

There was amusement in his eyes and although he looked tired and damp, he also looked more relaxed than she'd seen him in a while. The backpacking trip must have done him good.

While she fixed a plate for Zack, he showered. She set the microwave and turned it on, then went down the hall to his bedroom. She'd never been inside.

When she stepped over the threshold, she knew she was entering masculine territory. There was a smell of cologne and musk and man along with telltale signs of Zack's presence. A pair of navy flannel jogging pants were slung over the high-back wing chair. They were almost the same color as the fabric. The navy drapes at the windows looked as if they were made of a burlap material. She often used the loosely-woven fabric to decorate more masculine areas of houses. His triple dresser held a TV-VCR combination perched on one end. There was a man's valet in the center with his change and keys on top. To the right was a picture of Sherry Morgan holding an infant.

The truth was, Melanie felt like an intruder. She quickly rounded the four-poster pine bed and saw Zack's wet jeans, shirt, T-shirt and briefs mounded outside his bathroom door. The briefs gave her pause for a moment as she heard the shower running. Her mind conjured up images of Zack under it, and she felt hot just thinking about him there.

Enough of that, she warned herself, quickly hauling the clothes into her arms and hurrying out of his bedroom.

Zack dried off with a fluffy white towel and realized he hadn't brought any clothes into the bathroom with him. Opening the bathroom door, he saw that the wet clothes were gone. Good. That meant Melanie wasn't anywhere nearby.

But he'd no sooner exited the bathroom than she stepped over the threshold into his bedroom. They both stopped, frozen. Her gaze passed over him as if she couldn't help looking, as if she couldn't help being fascinated by what she saw. In those few moments, his body responded to the curiosity in her gaze as well as much more than that. He saw hunger, and he knew it matched the hunger he felt in himself.

Then suddenly she averted her eyes, spun around away from him and stammered, ''I'm...I'm sorry. I thought you'd still be in the bathroom or dressed. I wanted to know if Flo usually puts your jeans in the dryer and...and your supper's ready. I'll be in the kitchen...."

While she was stammering, he grabbed his jogging pants from the chair and slid into them. Tying the drawstring, he assured her quickly, "Melanie, it's okay. I'm dressed."

"Dressed?" She looked over her shoulder tentatively as if she didn't quite believe him. But then she saw that he was, in a manner, dressed.

"I should have knocked on the door frame or something—"

He took a few steps closer to her, and the remembrance of what she'd seen was in her eyes. "It's okay. Honest. Those kinds of things happen when people share living quarters."

"I'm sorry," she repeated. "I never expected—"

He took her by the shoulders. "Melanie, it's okay." He didn't know why she was so shaken up. Hadn't she ever seen a man naked before? Then he thought about what seeing her naked might do to him.

Geez.

He released her and decided the best thing was to treat what had happened matter-of-factly. "Flo does put my jeans in the dryer, and I'm glad supper's ready because I'm starved. I'll be out as soon as I find a clean T-shirt."

Her cheeks were redder than he'd ever seen them, and now her gaze looked as though it didn't know where to settle. It dropped to his bare chest, then to the waist of his pants, and then fluttered up to his eyes. But she couldn't meet them and she looked away.

Turning, she quickly headed for the door. "Milk or soda?" she tossed over her shoulder.

"Milk," he answered, but she was already out the door.

A few minutes later he entered the kitchen. They'd better smooth this over now or they wouldn't be able to work together. "Why don't you make yourself a cup of tea and keep me company?" he asked. He knew she liked tea. She had a cup almost every night before she went to bed—chamomile or something.

"Zack, I really should go to my room and work on—"

She still wasn't meeting his gaze, and now he clasped her elbow. "Come on. If you sit with me I'll tell you how many stars I counted while trying to go to sleep on my bedroll. If that's not fascinating enough, I'll try to give you an adequate rendition of three men snoring in a tent."

She smiled at that and finally faced him. "All right. I'll put some water on."

He kept his hand at her elbow, and she didn't move.

"Did everything go okay with Flo while I was away?" That wasn't what was on his mind, but would have to do for a starter.

"Sure. I like Flo a lot and I love helping her take care of Amy."

"Amy wasn't a bundle of trouble with Flo gone this evening?"

"She couldn't be trouble if she tried. We played patty-cake and built with blocks, made animal noises. Your usual nineteen-month-old activities."

There was laughter in Melanie's eyes, and he liked seeing it there. Sometimes she looked so serious. "Good, I'm glad you had fun with her. I always do, too."

Once more they shared a moment of complete understanding…so complete that Zack knew he had to ask her the question that had been on his mind since before he left. "Are you and Jordan Wilson involved?"

Melanie looked surprised at the sudden change of topic. Then she responded, "Jordan's a friend."

"How good a friend?" Zack asked.

"He helped me through a difficult time."

"Your accident?"

"And the aftermath of it. I relied on Jordan to keep me…steady. He was supportive while I was recovering, and he still is."

"You depend on him?" Zack didn't like that idea at all.

"Not as much as I used to. We're good friends, Zack."

Good friends who might become more? On the camping trip, he'd thought too much about Wilson and Melanie being together in more than a friendly way.

The temptation of her being so close was too hard to resist. He tipped her chin up. "Don't be embarrassed by what happened in the bedroom. It was just one of those things."

"Yes," she murmured. "Just one of those things."

As his thumb caressed her cheek, he moved a step closer.

The door to the penthouse banged shut and Flo called from the foyer, "Hello, everyone. I'm home."

Zack dropped his hand from Melanie's face and stepped away. His housekeeper had amazingly bad timing.

Chapter Six

Although Melanie was consulting with Zack's foreman on Wednesday about the type of subfloor they would need, she was still aware of Zack entering the work area. She hadn't seen him much since Sunday evening when Flo had interrupted whatever had almost happened between them. Melanie's embarrassment over seeing Zack naked hadn't quite dissipated, and whenever she closed her eyes, she could still see him clearly—the broad, muscled shoulders, the furring of dark hair on his chest, his lower body as he'd become aroused...

She tried to concentrate on the workman's words, still noticing, however, that Zack looked tired. He'd been spending long hours in his office since the backpacking trip, to make up for lost work time. Something about his coloring today troubled her. He left before she finished her conversation with his foreman, and she wondered if he'd be working in his office in the penthouse today rather than in Santa Rosa. In six weeks this would officially be his headquarters. It was hard to believe Thanksgiving was only a week away.

Melanie didn't see Zack again until she was helping Flo with supper. They heard the door to the penthouse open, followed by a clanging sound and a thump on the floor.

"Do you want to check or should I?" Flo asked with a smile. "It might be a noisy burglar."

With the penthouse's security system, Melanie knew that was unlikely. "I'll check."

When she reached the foyer, the door was wide open and two file-filled wooden drawers sat on the floor. Looking out into the hall, she heard the elevator returning to the penthouse floor. Zack stepped out, another of the heavy drawers in his arms.

She moved out of his way as he came in and asked in a teasing tone, "Isn't this a job for the movers?"

After he set the drawer down, he started to straighten. "I'll need these files here—" He broke off as he suddenly reached for the doorjamb.

Instead of looking gray as he had earlier in the day, he was flushed now and sweating.

"Zack? Are you okay?" Without thinking twice, she stepped close to him.

"I'm fine," he mumbled still hanging on to the doorjamb.

Peering up into his face, she knew he was anything but fine. "Are you having chest pains? Are you…?"

"Everything just spun for a moment," he said sharply. "I'm fine."

Her hand went to his forehead. He backed away, but the movement must have made him dizzy because he suddenly stilled.

"You're burning up!"

"I've been carrying the file drawers—" he grumbled.

"This has nothing to do with the files." Grabbing his arm, she tugged him toward the living room. "Come sit down."

When he didn't argue with her, she knew he really must be feeling rotten. "Stay still," she ordered. Then she hurried off to ask Flo where she kept the thermometer.

In a few moments Melanie returned with it. Zack was sitting on the sofa with his elbows on his knees, his head in his hands.

"Let me take your temperature," she requested.

He shook his head. "I don't want to know. I have too much to do."

His brown eyes had that glazed look of fever, and she knew better than to let him put her off. "Come on, Zack. Be reasonable."

He arched his brows at her. "Reasonable is a matter of perception."

"By the time we argue about this, we can know what your temperature is." Without giving him another chance to protest, she slipped the end of the thermometer into his mouth. "Don't bite it," she teased with a smile. It was one of the old-fashioned ones without the plastic cover.

He glared at her, but she just gave him a sweet smile. Finally he snatched it from his mouth. "That's long enough."

She wasn't sure it was, but she took it from him. "I'm not sure it *was* long enough, but it's already 102 degrees. When did this start?"

He raked his hand through his hair. "The sore throat started yesterday. It's nothing, Melanie."

"What other symptoms do you have besides the sore throat and dizziness?"

"No symptoms. I'm sorry I said anything." He started to rise to his feet, but the room must have spun because he sat down again.

Worry filled her and made her bolder. "You should go to bed, Zack."

"Like hell."

"That's exactly how you're going to feel if you don't take care of this."

Closing his eyes for a few seconds, he continued to argue. "I'm going to take a couple of aspirin, and that will be the end of it."

Exasperated, she moved aside. "Let me see you get up and walk to your room on your own steam."

"I never could resist a dare," he mumbled. But when he rose, he swayed. After he took a few steps, he reached for the wall.

"Stubborn male," she murmured as she slipped her arm around his waist so he could lean on her. When he didn't make a comeback or try to push her away, she knew he really did feel lousy.

Gently she prodded, "Please let me help you to your bedroom."

This time he didn't argue as she supported him during their trek to the bedroom. It was obvious he was trying not to put his weight on her. He wasn't the type of man to lean on anyone, and she knew that. Still, it was time he learned that even a man as strong as he was had to depend on someone.

They crossed into his room, and she remembered the other day—seeing him naked—and how she'd felt weak all over. This was different. They made it to the bed, and he sank down heavily on it.

"I hate this," he mumbled.

"Being sick?"

"Having anyone see me like this."

"It's just me and Flo. Do you want me to call a doctor?"

"No, I *don't* want you to call the doctor," he snapped.

"All right. Then I guess you're just going to have to let either me or Flo help you. Where are your pajamas?"

At her question, he gave her a sharp glance. "I don't *wear* pajamas."

"Fine. Then undress and I'll get you some juice, soup and acetaminophen."

At that his gaze came up to hers. "You make one mean nurse. But Flo would be even worse."

She wasn't sure whether he was giving in or not. "I'm not mean, just persistent. You simply haven't come up against it before. While I'm gone, don't try to sneak out or I'll sic Flo on you."

A wry smile tipped up the corners of his lips as she left the room.

As the evening wore on, she could tell Zack felt worse. He only ate a few spoonfuls of soup and didn't down much of the liquid. He said his throat was too sore. That worried Melanie. He was determined to put Amy to bed until Melanie reminded him that what he had could be catching. With that he'd settled back on the pillows on his bed and closed his eyes. She left him there, knowing rest was the best thing for him.

After she helped Flo with Amy, Melanie watched TV for a little while. Before Flo went to bed, she said, "I looked in on Zack. He's sleeping."

"I'll check on him before I turn in," Melanie assured her.

When the news was over, Melanie poured a glass of juice and took it to Zack's room. She found him shivering. The texture of his skin was much too dry, and he looked miserable.

His voice was raspy as he commanded, "Just go to bed, Melanie."

"Why is it men have to be so macho about illness?" she asked with exasperation as she set the juice on his nightstand.

Not expecting an answer, she went to the linen closet in the hall. There she found an extra blanket. Stuffed into a box with Ace bandages and peroxide, she also found a hot water bottle. Armed to help Zack whether he wanted to be helped or not, she filled the hot water bottle and took it with the blanket to his bedroom.

Going to the side of the bed, she lifted the covers.

"What are you doing?" he barked, grabbing them from her.

Ignoring his outburst, she tucked the hot water bottle in by his side. "This will help you get warm." He was wearing briefs, and she tried not to look at the rest of his body as she wrestled the covers from him and pulled them up to his chin. Then she unfolded the blanket on top of the spread.

"If this doesn't help, I saw a ceramic-tile hot plate in the kitchen. I can heat it, wrap it and put it at your feet. While you're lying there, think of a beach on a warm day and the sun on your body. It might help you get warmer quicker."

"Hocus-pocus," Zack mumbled, glaring at her as if she was the cause of his discomfort.

His words reverberated in her head as she warmed water in the microwave for tea.

She was convinced creative visualization wasn't hocus-pocus. She'd done extensive reading about it, especially when her eyes were healing. She'd wanted them to heal as fast as possible and tried everything, including vitamin supplements. As many doctors did these days, she believed the mind and body worked together in mysterious ways. This whole experience with the corneal transplants had taught her that.

Back in Zack's room a few minutes later, she noticed he seemed to be shivering less. She offered him the mug of tea. "I want you to drink it all."

"Melanie…"

"You need liquids, Zack, to help your body heal. Come on. It's not too strong, and I put a little bit of orange and cinnamon in. It'll slide right down."

Taking the mug from her, he eyed her over it. Then as if he decided fighting her took too much energy, he sipped at it slowly.

Only the dim light on the dresser glowed in the room. There was an intimacy about taking care of Zack that felt so right to Melanie.

Once he'd finished with the mug, she asked, "Do you want to try to sleep? Or should I make another cup?"

They stared at each other for a few moments until Zack admitted, "That felt good going down."

She wanted to crawl into bed beside him to warm him, stroke his hair away from his forehead, give him whatever comfort she could. Tea would have to do. "I'll make another cup. If you fall asleep while I'm gone, I'll set it on your nightstand."

But Zack wasn't asleep when she returned. He was

shivering less now as he took the mug from her a second time. "Either the hot water bottle or the tea is helping. I'm not as cold."

"Good. That's the idea. But I bet you still ache all over."

"You've had the flu?"

"A few times. I know sleeping's tough because when you move, your body hurts everywhere."

"I need a damn distraction," he growled, and reached for the bedside radio to switch it on.

"I can read out loud for a while, if you'd like."

"You have to get your sleep," he mumbled but his hand left the switch.

"I don't mind. Really. Not if it will help." She looked at the books over on his bookshelf and nodded to them. "What's your favorite?"

"Walden."

"All right." She slid the volume of Henry David Thoreau from the shelf, then settled in the armchair on the other side of Zack's bed. "Sip the tea and close your eyes and maybe you can fall asleep."

Instead of fighting her this time, he took a few more swallows, then set the mug aside. When he lay back against the pillows he winced, and she suspected his head probably hurt along with everything else. She began reading in a low voice and didn't stop until she'd finished ten pages. Then she looked over at Zack.

He'd stopped moving restlessly, and his breathing was even. He was asleep.

She knew she should go back to her own room, but she rarely had a chance to watch him unobserved. His forehead was broad, his eyebrows thick and dark, his nose had a slight bump in it. There were two small scars on his right cheek, and she wondered where he'd gotten them. His beard shadow was dark now, more stubble than shadow, but it couldn't hide his angular jaw. In a way she felt as if she had known Zack forever. Yet everything about knowing him seemed exciting and new, too. All of it was so confusing. Yet she wasn't confused about her deepening feelings for him and Amy. She just didn't know what was going to come of them.

Deciding to stay a bit longer, she curled on her side with her head against the chairback.

It was the middle of the night when she awakened and realized Zack was restless. It was as if he couldn't find a spot on the sheet to fit his body. He looked pale, and she bet if she put her hand to his forehead, his fever would be high.

When he saw she was awake, he murmured hoarsely, "Go to bed."

She ignored his command. Going around to the side of the bed, she lifted the covers and plucked out the hot water bottle. "Are you still cold?"

"Melanie, I don't want you here. I want to—"

"Be miserable in peace? I can understand that, but your fever's up again. Until it breaks you're going to feel like this, so we've got to make it break."

"It might have to run its course."

"Yes, it might. Do you want to be fighting the whole time it does? Save your strength, Zack. Just pretend I'm a nurse. I'll try to make you comfortable, then I'll leave. I promise."

She waited for his consent, and in a few moments he gave a slight nod.

Doing all the things she had done for him before, she tried to look at the situation clinically as she tucked the hot water bottle in by his side. Her fingers grazed his intensely hot skin, and she felt him suck in a breath. Their gazes met, and in spite of his fever, she could feel the sexual vibrations that always hummed between them.

After he'd downed two more pills and settled back on the pillow, she suggested, "Everything always seems worse in the middle of the night. In a few hours it'll be morning."

She turned to leave him then, to give him the peace he wanted, but to her surprise, he caught her hand. It was a firm but gentle clasp that let her know his strength was still there. "Thank you."

"You're welcome."

He released her hand slowly, but his gaze still held hers. She looked away first, afraid he would see too much.

It was 6:00 a.m. when Zack awakened. He could tell his fever had broken. The sheets were wet as was his pillowcase. He should change them. If not that, he should at least move over to the other side of the bed. He didn't feel as bad as he had last night, but he didn't feel strong enough to lift those file drawers again, either.

Before he could decide the best course of action, his bedroom door slowly opened and Melanie peeked in. He suspected she'd set her alarm so she could check on him. She looked sleep tousled and so very beautiful. He almost forgot how weak he'd felt a moment before. She was wearing a pink-flowered flannel robe, and he could see a pale blue nightgown underneath. Her robe didn't have buttons, and she'd belted it tightly.

She moved to his side, her brow creased in concern as she saw the sweat beading on his forehead. She touched the damp pillow. Her hand was so near his face. If he turned toward it, he could kiss her palm.

He must be delirious. "I just woke up."

"I'll change the sheets for you. Where's your robe?"

Last night he would have told her to go away.... He would have told her sleeping on the other side of the bed was fine. He would have done anything so she wouldn't see him like this. But this morning he didn't feel as if he had to put on a front, and that was odd. With Sherry, he'd felt as if he'd had to be strong all the time, could never show her any weakness, never show her any of his flaws. Somehow he felt that Melanie accepted him however he was. That should have made him feel more comfortable, but instead it disconcerted him greatly.

"My robe's in the closet."

She opened the door to his walk-in closet, saw the blue terry cloth on the hook and snatched it off. When she handed it to him, he threw back the covers.

Her eyes widened.

"Nothing you haven't seen before." After all, he was wearing briefs this time. Still, she looked just as embarrassed as when he hadn't been. It gave him some pleasure to rattle her. He almost grinned.

He offered to help her change the bed, but she gave him one of those looks women know how to give, and he settled in the chair to wait.

"How's the dizziness?" she asked him.

"Practically gone. It must have been the fever. I'll be back on my feet later today."

"Would it be so terrible if you took a day off to rest?" she asked reasonably.

"Resting isn't on my schedule."

She looked at him and was about to open her mouth to say something when he smiled at her. "Gotcha."

They both laughed.

After a trip to the closet in the hall, she plopped the fresh bed linens onto the mattress. Remaking the bed loosened the belt on her robe. As she fluffed the pillow, the garment opened slightly. The neckline of her nightgown was cut in a deep V, and Zack could just see the hint of the mounds of her breasts. He became filled with a heat that had nothing to do with the fever, at least not last night's.

Efficiently she turned back the covers of the bed she'd just made, then tightened her belt again. "It's all ready for you."

With feeling better, everything she was doing seemed intimate, seemed to arouse all his basic urges. He could imagine her in that bed with him, under him, both of them getting lost in the pleasure...

Pushing himself to his feet, he knew he had to thank her in some way for last night and wasn't sure quite how to do it. A gift didn't seem appropriate. Then he thought about the holiday next week.

"Do you have any plans for Thanksgiving?"

She looked startled. "No...I don't."

"I thought maybe you and Wilson—"

In a rush she assured him, "No. Jordan has family in San Diego. He spends the holidays with them."

Were she and Jordan Wilson just friends? Zack had hardly recognized the green-eyed monster that had bitten him when he'd seen her with the man. Now he wondered if she and Wilson were merely friends because that friendship simply hadn't developed into more...yet.

"Flo is taking time off over Thanksgiving to spend

with her sister, and Pop and I are going out to eat. Would you like to join us?"

Her smile was radiant. "Thank you, Zack. I'd like that. Are you sure your dad won't mind?"

"He won't care. In fact, he'll probably be glad. I'm sure you'll keep the conversation going better than I can." Then he remembered what he'd said to her about her not being a member of the family. He'd been wrong about that. She was feeling more and more like a member of the family every day.

He wasn't sure if that was good, or something he was going to regret.

Although Melanie was going out to dinner with Zack and Amy and Ted Morgan, she decided Thanksgiving just wouldn't be Thanksgiving without home-cooked food. So she made pumpkin pies and surprised Zack with them the evening before Thanksgiving.

He looked totally taken aback. "You didn't have to do that."

"I wanted to," she told him. "We can take these to your dad's. After dinner we can have them for dessert."

He looked as if he wanted to kiss her then. Yet both of them knew they were alone in the penthouse and Flo wouldn't be back until late on Friday. A kiss could tempt fate. A kiss could lead them both into something they weren't ready for.

On Thursday afternoon as they sat around Ted's kitchen table and Melanie added dollops of whipped cream to each of the pieces of pie, Zack's dad commented, "You look as if you're used to doing that."

"I've garnished a pie or two."

Ted's brows shot up. "You're not an interior decorator at all. You're a chef."

She laughed. "Nope, I just enjoy puttering around the kitchen."

Ted's gaze met his son's, and they exchanged a look that Melanie didn't understand.

Amy's idea of eating pumpkin pie was to smear whipped cream all over her face. Shaking his head, Zack took his daughter from her high chair. "I'm going to clean her up, then take her out for a walk. Anyone else interested in coming?"

Ted patted his full stomach. "No way. Just feel like being lazy today. Melanie can keep me company if you don't mind."

"Maybe Melanie would rather get some fresh air," Zack responded.

He was giving her an out in case she didn't want to be stuck in here with his dad. "I don't mind keeping your dad company. Maybe I'll even share some of the secrets of the kitchen with him."

Ted laughed. "You can share secrets all you want, but I think I'll need a few hundred lessons."

By the time Zack took Amy outside, Melanie and Ted moved to the living room with their cups of coffee. They engaged in small talk for a while until Ted asked her, "Do you really like to cook?"

"Yes, I do. It's not just the cooking. I love the smells, the way they make a home feel. Do you know what I mean?"

Studying her, Ted nodded. "I know exactly what you mean. After Zack's mom died..." He shook his head. "The kitchen was never the same place. The meals were just something you did. I was hoping when Zack married Sherry..." He stopped abruptly and gave her a sideways glance. "I was never very comfortable with Sherry."

Melanie held her breath. Was she finally going to find out something about Sherry Morgan and her life with Zack?

"She was one of those women who loved to get dressed up in a suit and high heels every day and bring home take-out for supper," Ted went on.

"She had a career?"

"Oh, yeah. A high-powered one. She was an executive in a cosmetics company. She was almost as driven as Zack to succeed."

"Do you think that's why they married? They were so much alike?"

Vigorously Ted shook his head. "I'm not sure how alike they were. Sherry came from a divorced home. Her mother always worked. Zack, on the other hand, knew what it was like to have his mom waiting for him when he got home."

"Most couples need both incomes nowadays," Melanie offered.

"Yeah, I guess. But with Sherry, work was more than a job. I think it meant more than Zack and even Amy. After Amy was born, she went into a real funk."

"Postpartum depression?"

"I don't know what it was called. She loved Amy. She just didn't want to be with her all day."

"And Zack knew that?"

"He couldn't help but know it. They made an agreement. When Amy was six months old, Sherry was going to go back to work and they were going to hire a nanny. A nanny," Ted scoffed.

"Flo is very good with Amy."

"Sure she is, like her grandmama. But no housekeeper or nanny is Amy's mother.'' He took a few swallows of coffee, and his cup rattled as he set it in the saucer. "You're good with Amy, too.''

"Amy's a wonderful little girl. I can't see how anyone wouldn't just want to cuddle her and love her anytime they're around her.''

"Are you going to stay with Zack until his offices open up?''

"That seems to be the most time efficient thing to do. I'll look for an apartment in Santa Rosa between Christmas and New Year's.''

"I bet Zack will miss you when you leave.''

Hopefully she'd be confiding in Zack before she left. Hopefully he would understand why she'd come to him this way and they'd still be friends when she moved into an apartment.

Friends? Maybe a lot more.

It was almost midnight. Zack sat in his office, the computer on, papers fanned out across his desk. He was having trouble concentrating. He was thinking about the day and how Melanie had turned Thanksgiving into something special with her pies. Last Thanksgiving had been terrible with his dad treading on eggshells, both of them not bringing up Sherry's name.

Today before they'd left, his father had said, "I like Melanie. She's something special. It's a shame she'll be moving out come January.''

He'd responded, "She has her own life. This is only temporary.'' Then Ted Morgan had looked at Zack with questions in his eyes, and Zack didn't have any of the answers.

Finally Zack studied the figures on the monitor and made himself concentrate on entering information into the computer. He'd been at it a few minutes when he heard Amy's cry.

Now and then she had bad dreams, and he always went to her to hold her and rock her back to sleep again. Pushing himself away from his desk, he stood and hurried to his daughter's room. But as he entered the hall, he saw a flash of pink and realized Melanie must have heard Amy, too. As he reached the doorway, he saw Melanie switch on the light and hurry to the crib. Her expression was worried—as if she knew what it was like for a child to have bad dreams. She wasn't aware of him on the threshold as she approached his baby.

"What's wrong, honey?" Melanie asked with so much gentleness and compassion in her voice that it gripped Zack and tightened his throat.

Amy pushed herself up with her little arms and then reached for Melanie. "Mommy!"

Melanie's face went white.

Zack stepped into the room, his heart aching and pounding at the same time. Melanie *wasn't* his daughter's mommy. Sherry was. But Sherry wasn't here.

He watched Melanie gather Amy into her arms, his mind racing. He didn't think Amy could possibly remember Sherry. Had she picked up the word *mommy* from having someone read to her...from watching TV? Was that possible at nineteen months?

And why did Melanie seem so shaken?

Chapter Seven

When Zack crossed the room to Melanie, she seemed startled to see him. She was still pale, but she gave him a small smile and said, "I heard Amy cry out."

Melanie wasn't wearing a robe. Her pale pink nightgown was edged in lace, the three-quarter-length sleeves full and feminine. The nightgown was gathered above her breasts, but he could still see the outline of them. Except for the dip of the V-neckline, there was nothing immodest about the gown. Yet he knew she probably wore nothing underneath. He felt himself growing hard, and the tension straining his body reminded him how long it had been since he'd touched a woman intimately, since he'd found satisfaction in sexual pleasure.

Amy had curled up against Melanie's shoulder and had closed her eyes, dozing off again. It took him aback because sometimes *he* had to rock her for an hour before she went back to sleep.

His gaze went from his daughter back to Melanie.

He found the paleness in her cheeks was gone and now they were a rosy red, as if she'd known what he was thinking as he looked at her.

"I just jumped out of bed and came right over when I heard her," she added softly.

"I heard her, too." He gently ran his forefinger down Amy's cheek. "It looks as if she's forgotten whatever troubled her dreams." Inhaling Melanie's sweet scent along with Amy's baby lotion, he suspected Melanie had taken a shower right before turning in. Her hair was tousled, soft and fluffy, and he wanted to feel it between his fingers. Maybe Amy's troubled dreams had passed, but he suspected his were just starting.

"Do you want me to put her back in her crib?" Melanie's blue eyes were filled with an emotion he didn't understand. Embarrassment because she was in her nightgown? Concern because Amy had called her mommy? No, something more than that. Something deeper than that.

"Go ahead and lay her down. Maybe she'll stay asleep."

When Melanie did as he suggested, his daughter curled up into a little ball, looking content and peaceful again.

He placed BoBo in the proper corner so Amy could find him easily if she awakened and wanted him. Then he kissed her forehead and, on his way out, switched off the light.

Melanie slipped past him into the hall. Before she could escape entirely, he'd eaten up the distance between them and stopped at her bedroom door. "Thanks for going in to her."

"I forgot you had the monitor in your office."

"They're a great invention. Sometimes I almost think I can hear her breathing."

"When I—" Melanie abruptly stopped.

"When you what?"

"N-nothing," Melanie stammered.

"Are you all right?" Zack asked. "You looked kind of pale. Maybe you're catching what I had."

"I feel fine, Zack. Really. Maybe it was just hopping out of bed so quickly."

Bed. Her bed…his bed…the two of them in it. Flo gone until tomorrow.

Forget it, Morgan. Blank those pictures right out of your head.

"Go back to bed," he said gruffly.

In a hurry before, she didn't move now. "What would you like for breakfast?"

They were standing so close, all he had to do was lean forward, and their arms would brush. Her breasts would be tantalizingly close to his chest. His voice was husky. "You don't have to make breakfast. I'll take care of it."

"I don't mind. I told Flo I'd watch over the two of you."

Realizing a kiss would take them right into her bedroom, he responded quickly, "We don't need anyone to watch over us."

"If you want to work tomorrow, I can keep Amy with me while I write up orders."

"She's *my* daughter, Melanie, and *my* responsibility. You just take care of the things you have to take care of and let me know if there are any glitches."

Looking taken aback by his brusqueness, she moved away from him into her bedroom. "I'll do that. Good night, Zack."

She didn't wait for his return good-night, but shut the door, taking temptation out of his reach…at least for tonight.

On Saturday afternoon Zack was closeted in his office when Melanie and Flo saw the first snowflakes falling. They took Amy to the window to look outside.

Since Thursday night, when Amy had called Melanie mommy, she'd felt an even stronger bond with the little girl. Did Amy know her mommy was somehow with her? Did she know that Melanie and her mommy were intertwined somehow? The knowing she'd seen in Amy's eyes had shaken Melanie, and she'd been afraid Zack would see how much. He'd glimpsed it, but she'd managed to explain it away. Now as she stood at the huge picture window in the living room where they seemed to be halfway to the sky, she felt such motherly feelings toward Amy, she didn't know if they were all hers. Whatever they were, she was cherishing them.

Amy pointed to the white flakes, giggled and tried to reach them through the window.

"We should take her outside," Melanie suggested.

"Oh, I can't. I have to watch what's in the oven. But I'm sure Zack wouldn't mind if *you* did. Go ahead and get her ready. I'll let him know."

"I won't keep her out long."

"She'll be seeing lots more snow after Christmas," Flo said. "Zack's planning a ski trip between Christmas and New Year's. I'm going along, too. While he skis, Amy and I will play in front of the fire."

Zack hadn't mentioned anything about the trip to Melanie. "It sounds nice."

"Do you have plans over Christmas?" the housekeeper asked.

Christmas. Melanie had just tried to get through it last year. She was hoping this year would be different. She hadn't really thought about it yet because thinking about it brought too much pain.

"No. No plans. I'll be getting Zack's offices ready for the grand opening."

Flo looked outside to see if the snow was still falling. "You'd better get out there before it stops. It might not last long."

Fifteen minutes later Melanie was outside on a grassy area beside the garage holding Amy while they both lifted their faces up to the sky. The gentle flakes seemed to float down in slow motion. Amy giggled as they landed on her nose and cheeks.

Melanie said, "Stick out your tongue and try to catch them that way." Then she did it so Amy could see how.

Amy thrust out her little tongue, and a snowflake landed on it. She laughed gleefully, waving her arms at the sky. "More," she demanded, and then did it again.

Melanie's heart filled to overflowing with this little bundle of joy in her arms. Then suddenly she was aware that they weren't alone. A sixth sense where Zack was concerned told her he'd come outside and was watching them. She felt foolish now, tasting the snow.

When Zack stepped outside, he wished he had a camera. The pure enjoyment on Melanie's and Amy's faces was something to behold. Melanie was teaching his daughter to enjoy life the way she did...fully, taking pleasure in little things.

Melanie looked over at him, like a little girl who'd been caught doing something foolish. He grinned at her.

"She loves it," Melanie murmured.

His daughter was trying to catch the snowflakes as they fell. Realizing she had nothing in her hand, but that the ground was turning white, she said, "Down, down, down," to Melanie, pointing to the dusting of white on the grass.

Melanie looked at Zack to see if it was all right with him. "Sure, let her down. We're not going to be out here that long."

As soon as Amy was on the ground, she squatted down, trying to pinch the snow between her fingers. She was fascinated by it, and Zack chuckled. She saw a spot on the grass a few feet away where there was more of the white fluff and scurried over there, hunkering down again.

"Wouldn't you just like to frame that picture in your mind and never forget how she looks?" Melanie asked.

"That's exactly what I was thinking when I came outside—about both of you."

Melanie's gaze met his and she looked surprised, but then she blushed. "Kind of a childish thing to do."

"Not so childish. It was more sensual than anything." Though he'd been thinking it all along, now he realized he'd spoken the words aloud.

Maybe it was the remembrance of the flakes on her tongue, but Melanie ran her tongue over her upper lip, and Zack felt his body respond.

Amy was still occupied with the snow and the blades of grass. Standing there, white floating around them, Zack felt as if he was in one of those snow globes with nothing quite real. But the desire he felt for Melanie was very real. Acting on impulse, he slid his hand to the nape of her neck and into her hair. She stared up at him, her blue eyes wide. He bent his head and kissed her. His lips on hers created such heat, he thought the snow would stop right then and there. As he slid his tongue into her mouth, he felt her gasp of pleasure and took advantage of it.

Then as quickly as he'd begun the kiss, he ended it. "I wanted to taste the snowflakes on your lips."

"Did you?" she asked, looking a bit dazed.

"I tasted your excitement, your appreciation of something as simple as a snowflake. When I'm with you, I see the world differently."

"Is that good or bad?" she whispered.

"Neither. Just unsettling. You're unsettling," he said honestly.

Amy straightened and ran to a patch of snow that had settled on a cedar. She touched it and turned around to look at Zack as if she'd found the most wondrous treasure.

"I don't mean to unsettle you," Melanie said softly.

Again he was caught by the blue of her eyes and the expression in them. "Do *I* unsettle *you?*"

"Yes."

That one-word admission pleased him. Maybe he should stop fighting the idea of enjoying the chemistry between them. They were adults. What could it hurt? "I'm going over to Pop's tomorrow to put up Christmas lights. He's going to order a pizza. Would you like to come along?"

She hesitated a moment before asking, "Are you sure I wouldn't be intruding?"

"Positive. You can keep Pop occupied so he stays out of my hair while I'm doing it. I've put up his lights every year for the past five years, and he still wants to tell me how to do it every step of the way."

Just then Amy decided to take off toward the corner of the building to explore from a different vantage point. Zack saw her, ran after her, scooped her up and hoisted her onto his shoulders. "See if you can reach the sky and catch a couple of handfuls."

She did as he suggested, her face turned up, her hands reaching toward heaven.

When he glanced at Melanie, he thought he saw tears in her eyes, but it must have been the cold and the snow.

Proving she must be cold, she said, "I'll go in and make hot chocolate. It'll be ready when you and Amy have caught enough snowflakes."

Before he could look into her eyes again, she'd turned away from him and was walking toward the building. Maybe he'd been wrong to ask her to go along to his dad's. She fitted into his life too easily. It was almost as if she'd always been a part of it.

Was he thinking about really getting involved again?

No. Sherry had shattered his trust when she'd spoken of an abortion and not wanting their second child. That had been a tear in the fabric of their marriage. If she had lived, they might never have been able to mend it. He didn't think he'd ever be able to trust a woman to want the same things he did in life.

But that didn't mean he couldn't enjoy Melanie Carlotti's company without getting involved, without taking the risk of putting his heart on the line again.

Yesterday's snow had stopped soon after it started. Melanie couldn't forget the heat of Zack's lips on hers in the midst of the cold. She'd felt warm for hours. Was he finally accepting the chemistry between them? Is that why he'd invited her to his father's today? Or did he just want a buffer between him and Ted Morgan so the tension wouldn't get out of hand?

Ted looked genuinely glad to see her when she arrived with Zack and Amy. "Aren't you a sight to pretty up a man's house!"

"Some women would take that as an insult, Pop," Zack remarked wryly.

His father looked dismayed, and Melanie was quick to assure him, "I know that was a compliment and I thank you for it." She lifted the bag in her hand, "And I didn't come empty-handed. Zack said you were going to order pizza. I have a salad and some cookies Flo made."

"That's terrific. Then we won't have to snitch any of Amy's applesauce."

Melanie laughed, but Zack just rolled his eyes. The two men were definitely of different generations and on different wave lengths, but she understood and appreciated both of them and wished Zack could see that his dad meant well.

While Zack found everything he needed in the attic, Melanie told Ted about Amy's reaction to the snow. When he questioned his granddaughter about the white stuff, she said, "Cold. Wet."

"That about sums it up," he agreed with a laugh.

After Zack tested the lights, he took them outside while she and Ted conversed about the age of his house, how long he'd lived in the neighborhood, and 101 other details that had shaped Zack's life. Ted regaled her with Zack's exploits as a kid, and she was glad Zack was outside because he certainly would have stopped his father and she wanted to hear everything.

Amy had soon emptied the laundry basket full of toys Ted kept in a corner for her. She was happily playing with a musical top when Ted peered out the window and frowned. "I hope Zack is careful on that ladder. It's kinda wobbly."

"I'll go out and check on how he's doing. If he'll let me, I'll hold it steady."

"That's the problem with my son," Ted said. "He doesn't let people help him. He's had a hard time since Sherry died, but he doesn't want anybody to see it."

"That's not unusual, Mr. Morgan."

"Ted," he reminded her again.

She smiled and repeated, "Ted." Then her smile slipped away as she added, "It's hard to talk about loss. It seems to make it that much more real."

Zack's father tilted his head and studied her. "It's a blessing you dropped into my son's life. Maybe you can get him living again."

She slipped into her coat. "Right now, maybe I can just hold his ladder steady."

The temperature had gone up to around forty, but there was wind today and it seemed to penetrate Melanie's royal-blue light wool coat. If she was going to stay in this area of California, she'd have to buy a heavy jacket.

When she stepped outside, she turned to her left where Zack's ladder was propped against the chimney. She gazed up at him as he worked, admiring the way his jeans fit, thinking he looked rugged in the flannel shirt and insulated red vest. "Your dad said the ladder's rickety. Do you need me to steady it for you?"

"The ladder's fine as long as I have it on solid ground. You could stand out a ways, though, to see if I've gotten this straight."

Melanie stepped back a few feet and gazed up at the angel Zack had attached to the brick chimney. "Her trumpet's pointing toward the stars. She looks good to me. Are you going to put blue lights in the middle of the roof and white lights on the sides?"

Zack didn't answer her, and when she looked up at him, she saw that he looked as if he was chiseled out of granite. Finally he asked, ''Why would you suggest that?''

Taking a deep breath, Melanie realized that for an instant she'd seen the house the way it had been when Sherry was alive. ''I...I thought the combination would look pretty with the angel and all.''

Zack descended the ladder and crossed to her. ''The year after Sherry and I were married, she decided Pop should use blue lights in the middle and white lights on the sides.''

''What a coincidence.'' For a moment Melanie thought about telling Zack everything. But he was on alert, on guard, and she knew with every fiber of her being that he wouldn't accept what she had to tell him. Not yet.

She added, ''I guess it's not so unusual that angels make us think of heaven and stars—blue and white light.''

''I suppose not,'' he said gruffly, though his gaze was still probing as he looked for answers to questions not yet formed. Abruptly he stared again at the angel.

A blast of cold air made Melanie shiver. She wrapped her arms around herself.

''You'd better go in. Your coat isn't warm enough for this kind of weather.''

Glad to be off the subject of the lights, Melanie stuffed her hands into her pockets. ''I think I'll go into Santa Rosa this week to one of the malls and buy something heavier.''

It would be a quick trip. The stores would be decorated for Christmas. She didn't want to spend too much time in them. Bright balls, glittering tinsel and holiday trappings reminded her too much of everything she'd lost. The holidays brought back so many feelings and memories she was trying to keep in a sealed box until she felt strong enough to deal with them. Would she ever be strong enough to deal with them?

"Tell Dad to order the pizza in a half hour," Zack suggested, breaking into her thoughts. "By the time it gets here, I should be finished."

Knowing it was best if she went inside, hoping another of Sherry's memories didn't come popping out of her mouth, she simply responded, "Amy's going to love it when you're finished."

"She's old enough to like everything about Christmas this year." Then he moved toward the ladder once more, leaving Melanie with thoughts of her own daughter and pictures in her mind that would never fade.

On Monday evening after supper, Flo had taken Amy into the living room to play. Zack had been about to sit down on the floor with his daughter, to spend the evening with her, when the phone rang.

He said to Flo, "I'll pick it up on the cordless in the kitchen. I'm expecting a call from one of my distributors."

When he reached the kitchen, he saw the phone wasn't there and realized it had stopped ringing. Sometimes Melanie took the handset back to her bedroom to make calls. She must have done that tonight. Still thinking the phone call might be for him, he went down the hall to her bedroom. Her door was partially open, and he stopped when he realized the call was for her.

"Yes, this is Melanie Carlotti. Oh, hello Mr. Kellison."

Zack recognized the name of the reporter he'd met

at Cecile and Don's. Why was Tom Kellison calling Melanie? Maybe he wanted her point of view on the office complex.

He realized otherwise when he heard Melanie say, "Yes, I'm that Melanie Carlotti. But I don't want you to do a follow-up article. Everything that happened is too painful. Please don't pursue it."

Zack recalled their conversation with Tom. Tom had thought he'd recognized Melanie's name, but she'd pushed that idea aside.

Zack thought again about yesterday, the way she'd seemed to know what color lights went on the front of his dad's house. A fluke? And what about that letter she'd received from the private investigator? Now it seemed her name had appeared in the newspaper for some reason. Whatever the situation, it had been important enough for a reporter to want to do a follow-up. The accident she mentioned? The one she wouldn't talk about?

All of it added up to some kind of secret. Tomorrow he'd go to the library in Santa Rosa, do some sleuthing and maybe find out what Melanie was keeping from him.

The following afternoon Zack went through the most recent issues of the *L.A. Times*, not expecting to find anything. Then switching to the microfilm machine, he went back a year. Page by page he looked for references to accidents or to Melanie's name. He kept going back farther and farther, almost giving up, when finally he spotted the headline in December two years ago: Christmas Tree Fire Kills Father And Daughter.

The name Carlotti jumped out from the article and Zack read with horrified fascination. Apparently the

Carlottis' Christmas tree had caught fire while Melanie
was at a neighbor's. The neighbor's name was Barbara
Adair, the woman he'd called for Melanie's reference.
Melanie's husband, Phil, and their four-year-old daughter Kaitlyn had been asleep in the house. A passerby
had alerted everyone at the Adairs' party to a fire next
door. Melanie had run from the party straight to her
house, oblivious to the danger. When she'd opened the
front door, oxygen rushed in and fed the fire, shattering
the windows. Melanie was knocked unconscious and
injured by the shattered glass.

The scars Zack had seen at her temple. Where else
did she have scars? How badly had she been injured?
How devastating her loss—both her husband and
daughter. No wonder she'd seemed so understanding of
his pain. No wonder she seemed wise beyond her years.
Why hadn't she told him? Why couldn't she confide in
him?

He understood the kind of pain she must be feeling.
He also understood not wanting to relive it any more
than she had to. He'd told her Sherry had been in an
accident, but he'd never told her how or why because
he didn't want to go there. He didn't want to go back
and remember. He didn't want the guilt to overtake him
any more than it already had.

Did Melanie feel guilt, too? From what he knew
about fires, he suspected her husband and daughter had
already been dead before she opened that door. But
she'd caused the explosion, and she was still alive.

So many questions clicked through his mind. What
kind of marriage had she had? How long had she been
married? Had her daughter been everything to her as
Amy was to him? Certainly the way Melanie cared for
Amy, he suspected that was true.

After thinking about it, he made a copy of that page of the paper. He would never have known about it if he hadn't overheard her phone conversation.

Yet he knew he wasn't going to bring it up to her. He wanted her to tell him about it.

When he asked himself why, he realized he wanted Melanie Carlotti to trust him...because he was beginning to care about her, more than he'd cared about anything since Sherry died.

Chapter Eight

Every year Zack hosted a Christmas dinner for his employees at the Fairmont Hotel in Santa Rosa. It was a tradition. Store managers, sales clerks and his executive officers all mingled. Usually it was like a family having a reunion once a year, and he enjoyed it as much as his employees. This year he'd extended an invitation to Melanie, too, and asked her to accompany him.

It had been more than two weeks since he'd found out about the fire that had taken Melanie's husband and daughter from her. Whenever they were together, either working or caring for Amy, he'd hoped Melanie would tell him something about her background, about the accident and everything that had happened to her. He was amazed at how much he wanted her to trust him. Maybe tonight she would. Maybe after spending the evening together... Pictures of the two of them doing *more* than talking had been distracting him for weeks.

As he guided Melanie into the Fairmont's huge ballroom, he decided she'd never looked prettier or more sensual. She was wearing a silky black dress that came almost to her ankles. It fastened with white-satin-covered buttons down the front and there were white satin cuffs on the long sleeves. Her patent leather high heels brought her head almost to his chin. She looked like dynamite tonight and beside her, with his hand in the small of her back, he was proud that he was escorting her.

She smiled up at him as he guided her toward a round table at the front of the room. "You have a great turn-out."

"It's a free meal," he said wryly.

She looked around at the groups of people talking, noting everyone who waved at Zack as he'd come through the crowd. "I think it's more than that. You apparently run a well-satisfied ship."

"I try to be fair. When we're doing well, I like to share that with everyone. For the long haul, if my employees are happy and my turnover's limited, my profits go up."

"You're a good man, Zack."

There was admiration in her eyes, and it did something to him. Sure, it made him feel ten feet tall. But it also intensified his desire for her. The way she looked tonight, the increasing closeness he felt toward her, was stoking the fire inside of him, and he didn't know how long he could contain it.

He led her to a table where his executive officers were seated. Melanie soon joined in the conversation as if she'd known everyone long before tonight.

She fits into your life so well.

The thought startled him and he realized he was considering getting involved with her. That's why he was giving her a different type of bonus from everyone else in his employ.

The band began playing during dinner. After a superb meal of prime rib, followed by coffee and an ice cream ball covered with coconut, Zack looked over at Melanie and asked, "Would you like to dance?" He'd been waiting all night to hold her in his arms.

"I'd love to." From the sparkle in her blue eyes, he knew she meant it.

There were already couples on the dance floor. Zack paid them no mind as he took Melanie into his arms.

"I love this song," she said as a romantic ballad from the eighties played.

"They don't seem to write them like that anymore."

The dreamy music wound around them, and Zack pulled her a little closer. Melanie didn't protest, and he found himself letting go of her hand and putting both arms around her.

"You look beautiful tonight," he murmured, his lips at her temple. He felt the slight shiver that ran through her. "Are you cold?" he asked.

She tipped her chin up. "No, I—I'm just enjoying you holding me."

So damn honest. That was one of the things he liked so much about Melanie. No games. No pretense. She usually said what she thought, and he didn't have to wonder what was going on with her. The idea that she liked him holding her as much as he liked holding her—

He passed his hands up and down her back in a caress that told her he'd like to do more than hold her. "If these were strangers all around me, I'd kiss you."

He didn't want to intentionally start gossip among his employees or put Melanie's reputation in jeopardy.

"You're thinking about my reputation," she murmured, reading his mind.

"Maybe I'm thinking about *my* reputation."

She laughed. "Somehow I doubt that."

Suddenly he needed to make something clear to her. "I don't have a reputation, Melanie. I mean, everyone here knew me as a happily married man and since Sherry's accident, I haven't dated."

"And you don't want everyone here to think we're paired together."

She'd read him all wrong. "I don't care about that. I just want you to know, one-night stands have never been a pastime for me."

Her expression was serious. "I never thought they were."

There was that understanding between them again...a bond that seemed to go deeper than the almost two months he'd known her. They seemed to have a lot in common. They seemed to care about the same things. He thought about her bonus in his pocket, the two of them curled up in front of a fireplace....

He brought her into his chest, very close, and gently kissed her temple. When the song ended, he was sorry.

His arms still around her, he explained, "We can dance again in a little while. I have to act as emcee for a few minutes."

Zack escorted Melanie back to their table, then crossed to the band leader and stepped up onto the stage, mike in hand. After a few opening remarks, he told his employees how happy he was to have them with him, to be working with them toward the same goal, making Sports & More a success.

A man from a table at his left rose and came toward him on the stage. It was his manager from the Santa

Rosa store, John Finney. He'd been in Zack's employ since Zack opened his first store.

John was holding something in his hand and now he climbed up on the stage with it, grinning. "May I borrow the mike?" he asked jokingly.

With a shrug and arched brows, Zack handed it over.

John was in his fifties with dark hair and black-rimmed glasses. He'd gained about twenty pounds since Zack had known him, but he'd gotten wiser with age and even more efficient. John held up the oak plaque in his hand. "We have something for you this year. It's the Best Boss Award."

Zack could see Best Boss engraved at the top and then three columns of names.

"Everyone of us wanted our names on this," John explained, "because we're proud to be working with you. Not only that," he said, striving for a bit of levity, "but your bonuses are the best around." Then he presented Zack with the plaque.

Zack didn't know what to say. John knew exactly how difficult the past fifteen months had been and had filled in where needed and never complained. He always had a listening ear for Zack to unload, and he was the most supportive employee Zack had. Extending his hand, he shook John's, and they exchanged a look that passed for a volume of words.

After John left the stage, Zack said a quick thank-you, told everyone to enjoy the night as long as they wanted and wished them a very merry Christmas.

When he returned to the table, he saw that Melanie's eyes were shining. She absolutely shimmered tonight and as he sat beside her, he took an envelope from his pocket. "I have a bonus for you, too."

She looked surprised. "I'm not a regular employee."

He shrugged. ''That doesn't matter. Besides, this is a special bonus and if you prefer a monetary one to this, just say so.''

Melanie looked puzzled as she took the envelope from him and their fingers brushed. Neither of them jerked away. He thought her fingers trembled slightly when she opened the envelope, but he couldn't be sure. She pulled out a colorful, trifold flyer for a ski resort near Redding and looked up at him perplexed.

''Flo, Amy and I are leaving for Winter Haven on the twenty-seventh and are coming back December 30. I made reservations for you, too. You'd have your own chalet and the three of us will be next door. Do you ski?''

''I haven't for a few years. But I do love it. Oh, Zack, this is wonderful. Are you sure you want me along? I mean, if this is a vacation for you with Amy…''

He knew she was remembering the comment he'd made about her not being a member of the family. ''I want you along. That's why I'm inviting you. Will you come?''

She gave him a wide smile. ''If we were in a room of strangers, I'd give you a big hug.''

''I'll collect it later.'' It was a promise, and he knew he wanted much more than a hug or a kiss from Melanie Carlotti.

As Zack drove back to the penthouse, Melanie felt buoyant, headily alive. She was aware of Zack glancing over at her often, aware of her own exhilarating heart rate every time he did. The quivering inside her hadn't let up since the moment Zack had taken her into his arms in the ballroom. She'd felt like Cinderella tonight. She'd felt as if she was on a date, and though Zack hadn't called it that, that's what it was. So much more than a date, too. Zack wanted her to share the holidays with them. He wanted her in his life.

After Zack parked in the garage, he came around to her door and took her hand as she alighted from his car. Neither of them spoke, as if they were afraid they'd break the spell that had wrapped them in a new closeness. Zack held on to her hand as they walked to the elevator. In a few short minutes they were standing inside the penthouse.

Melanie began to unbutton her coat, not sure what to say or do next.

Zack easily took care of that by asking, "How about a nightcap? I have a bottle of brandy that John gave me last year."

"That sounds nice." Anything with Zack sounded nice.

"It's in my office. I'll get it and meet you in the living room."

Melanie hardly had time to take a few deep breaths until Zack was towering above her, holding out a snifter of brandy to her. The amber liquid was an excuse for them to spend more time together tonight. She took it, waited for him to be seated next to her, then tried a sip.

"What do you think?" he asked.

"Very smooth."

He took a few sips of his own and set the glass on the coffee table beside hers. His brown eyes were darker than the brandy and much more intoxicating as he gazed at her and asked, "Did you enjoy yourself tonight?"

"Very much. Did you hear the buzz about your new offices? John's wife said she can't wait for the open house. Your store manager in Ukiah said the same thing.''

''I told John about Vincente Largo's sculpture. He was impressed. I assured him he'll be even more impressed when he sees what you've done with the executive office suites.'' Zack paused then added, ''I'd like to ask you a favor.''

''What?''

''Will you hostess the open house?''

''I'd be honored to do that with you.''

''Good.''

He was gazing at her with that same look of desire she'd glimpsed when they were dancing. The moment seemed suspended in time. ''I'd like that hug now.'' His voice was a husky command.

Everything inside of her was answering yes, yes, yes to the hunger and need glowing in his eyes. When she reached for him, he reached for her. Melding with a rustle of her dress and his low murmur of her name, they held each other long enough for the beats of their hearts to unify, long enough to realize hugs weren't enough, long enough for their breaths to quicken and their longing to become obvious to each other. His lips took hers with a need and hunger that had built up all evening, along with the desire she'd seen in his eyes, with a growing sense that he was letting her into his life. His tongue swept her mouth, engaging her in an exciting dance of man and woman. The lingering taste of brandy on both of their tongues added to all the delicious sensations as her fingers slipped into his hair, as she reveled in everything that was Zack and the moment and the fulfillment of her dreams.

Slowing the kiss, he brought his hands to her face and reluctantly pulled away from her. ''Tell me about your life before you came here. Tell me…about your accident.''

The passionate haze that had overtaken her cleared with his words. She wanted to tell him only the truth, but she knew she couldn't do that yet. Everything had become more complicated with this new closeness, and she was even more afraid now of him pushing her away…of him pushing her out of his life. The moment of truth was coming, but she needed to ward it off as long as possible to give his feelings time to grow so that they'd have a chance at the happiness she knew they could have.

Where did that knowing come from? Sherry?

She didn't want to think about Zack's wife now.

''Zack, can't we just live in the present?'' She wanted to forget her reason for coming here, forget that she was on a mission. She just wanted to go with the flow of the feelings that she knew she had for Zack and revel in the rightness of it.

Smoothing his thumb over the scar at her temple, he leaned forward and pressed a kiss there. ''We can try.''

Then she was in his arms and he was kissing her again.

Their kisses became so hungry that Melanie didn't even realize Zack had tugged off his tie and was now unfastening the buttons of her dress. This was what she wanted, wasn't it? Zack and now and satisfying a need that had begun with her dreams.

When he saw her black satin bra, he groaned, then traced his finger along the top of the half cups. ''Do you have any idea of how perfectly beautiful you are?''

The look in Zack's eyes told her he was speaking his truth. ''I feel beautiful when you look at me like that.''

"Like I can't wait to undress you?" His smile was sexy and made her tummy somersault.

"Is that what it means?"

His expression turned serious. "That and a lot more. I need you, Melanie."

She wanted more than his need, but that would have to do for now. "I need you, too," she murmured, wishing she could tell him she loved him, wishing she could tell him everything. Yet *everything* was too great a risk, especially at this moment.

When he kissed her again, it was tender, fiery, filled with a desire they'd shared but had restrained all these weeks. The weight of his lower body was tantalizingly erotic, but as he moved on top of her, she was restricted by her dress. It was a delicious restraint as his trousers moved against the silky material. She could feel his arousal, and her own sense of wanting grew until it seemed to fill the whole room.

Zack's hands explored as he kissed. As his tongue outlined her lips, his hand moved from her waist up her midriff so teasingly slowly. She pushed her tongue into his mouth wanting more, wanting faster, wanting all of Zack.

Accepting her passion, he stroked her tongue with his, but still didn't hurry, still moved his fingers over her skin as if he were memorizing every inch. When his hand reached her breasts, she thought she'd die from needing him to touch her. Still he teased, still he took entirely too much time, still he made a slow circle around her breast with his fingertips until she was writhing under him, kissing him with a fervor she never felt before...pleading in every silent way for him to truly make love to her.

When she opened her eyes for a moment, she saw

his were closed. The after-midnight silence intensified everything that was happening between them.

Breaking the kiss, he ran his lips down her neck and paused at the pulse at her throat. "Oh, Sherry," he murmured.

The wonderful, beautiful, heart-altering haze suddenly lifted with Zack's mention of his deceased wife's name. Melanie froze, hurt beyond measure, trying to understand, knowing reason had nothing to do with any of this. She went still and cold, and tears came to her eyes.

Zack must have realized immediately what he'd done, what he'd said. He pulled back, and she couldn't bear to look at him.

"I'm not Sherry," she murmured.

"Melanie, I'm sorry."

What was she doing here? How did she ever think he would come to love her. Did he sense Sherry was still with them...with her? Why had this burden come with such a wonderful gift?

She pushed at his shoulders, still avoiding his gaze. "Let me up, Zack."

"Melanie, it was a slip of the tongue. It was habit. It was…"

"It was all the things you still feel for her, might always feel for her."

Shaking his head and levering himself up, he protested, "You don't understand."

She swung her legs over the side of the sofa. As he ran his hand through his hair, she pleaded, "Help me understand, Zack."

His face was etched with the grief and recriminations of the past fifteen months. "Sherry and I had an argument before she died. She..." With a loud oath, he stood. "I want to turn the clock back."

She buttoned her dress. "You can't do that, Zack."

"Don't you think I know I can't? It's going to take time. I need to replace the old memories with better ones."

Her hands stilled as she realized he couldn't move forward in his life until he settled the past. "You can't just wipe out old memories as if they don't exist. Tell me what's troubling you so." Please help me understand why I'm here.

"Talking isn't going to change anything. I'm sorry about what happened, Melanie. I can only imagine how I'd feel if the situation was reversed."

Disappointment and sadness filled Melanie. He wasn't going to confide anything about his marriage or his feelings concerning Sherry. He wanted to stay in the here and now, and they couldn't do that without dealing with the past. One thing Melanie knew—she wasn't going to let him use her as a substitute or as a temporary bandage over a deep wound that needed work to heal. She was absolutely sure she loved Zack separately from whatever memories and feelings his wife had had. Right now, she wished she could make the dreams as well as everything else that seemed to come from Sherry just go away. She couldn't deny what was happening to her...to Zack...to both of them. More than anything she wished she had the answers to all of her questions and now realized she possibly never would.

Zack was still looking at her with that longing in his eyes, and she wanted to ease it. But she couldn't. Not this way.

She finished buttoning her dress, still feeling all the places on her body Zack's lips and hands had touched.

She tingled from his desire and hers. Desire was such a fleeting thing compared to everlasting love. What she felt with Zack was so much stronger than anything she'd ever felt with Phil.

When she stood, Zack did, too. Looking chagrined, he gazed into her eyes and didn't move away. "Don't let tonight influence whether or not you come on the ski vacation with us. I know Amy wants you there." Then he added, "I do, too."

Somehow they had to work this out. Somehow she had to find a way to talk to him about her dreams and Sherry. "I want to come along."

He looked relieved. "Good."

The awkwardness between them couldn't be banished with a few words, and they both knew it. Nothing they said could change what had happened. She stepped away from him, from what had happened on the sofa, needing to be alone right now. "I'll see you in the morning."

She felt Zack's eyes on her back as she left the room.

On Sunday afternoon Melanie was curled in a corner of the sofa catching up on her favorite decorating magazines when the intercom from the outside entrance buzzed. She went into the foyer to answer it. When she pushed the button, she expected one of Zack's friends or Flo's sister to be downstairs. But instead she heard Jordan's voice.

"I'm here to see Melanie Carlotti. Jordan Wilson."

"Jordan! What are you doing here?"

"Beam me up and I'll tell you."

Laughing, she said, "I'll unlock the door. Come on up."

After Melanie released the automated lock on the

outside entrance, she waited at the penthouse door. When Jordan stepped off the elevator, she saw he had a brightly wrapped package in his hands—a Christmas present.

For the most part, she'd managed to stave off the holidays, not letting herself think about them too often...or too much. Now here Jordan was, reminding her Christmas wasn't something she could ignore.

"Come on inside," she murmured, suddenly overcome by memories of Christmases past and pictures of Kaitlyn filling her head.

Jordan studied her carefully. "I was surprised when you answered the intercom instead of Mrs. Briggs."

She swallowed the lump in her throat. "Zack and Amy and Flo went to visit Zack's friends near Clear Lake. They asked me to go along, but..."

He looked worried now. "Is something wrong?"

After a sigh she admitted, "Everything is getting complicated. I just needed some time alone."

"Or time away from Zack?"

That was exactly what she'd needed. "I'm afraid I'm going to make a mess of all of this. I'm wondering if I should leave when this project's done without telling him anything." She really had been considering that since last night and the fiasco after they'd returned from his employee dinner.

"Can I get you something?" she asked Jordan. "Flo made cookies and I can brew up some hot chocolate."

"That sounds great."

Ten minutes later they were sitting on the sofa in the living room, sipping at mugs of chocolate.

"You took a chance coming without calling," she told him.

"It was a beautiful day for a drive. I can't stay long.

I have to check on two admissions at the hospital to-night. I wanted to give you this.'' He picked up the package he had brought with him and set it on her lap.

Melanie tore off the bow and then the wrappings. After she removed the lid of the box and brushed back the tissue paper, she found a mahogany framed découpage with dried pansies and roses arranged around a calligraphy saying.

Spring is just around the corner,
Hope is just around the bend.
The future is yours,
Define and claim and tend.

With Jordan knowing everything she'd been through and why she was here, she couldn't keep tears from welling in her eyes. ''Oh, Jordan, it's beautiful. And just what I need right now.''

''I knew the holidays would be difficult for you.''

''I don't want them to be.'' She brushed a stray tear away. ''I make myself remember them, and I see Kaitlyn as she sat under the tree with her new tricycle, with her new doll.'' After pausing, she added, ''She took her first steps at Christmas. Her eyes were always so bright with the wonder of it. But the memories aren't enough, and I miss her so desperately.'' The tears were falling too fast to blink away now.

Jordan hugged her, holding her tightly enough that she realized he knew exactly how she was feeling.

She was so lost in what had been and maybe what could be that she was hardly aware of the penthouse door opening. Needing Jordan's comfort, it took a few moments for the sounds to register, and by the time they did, Zack and Flo were standing in the doorway. Amy came running into the room.

The toddler tugged on Melanie's arm. "Mellie, Mellie. Saw horsey."

Flo disappeared down the hall as Melanie tried to compose herself, to bring herself back to the here and now, to remember she felt a bond with this little girl, too. She was swiping away the tears in her eyes by the time Zack got to Amy and scooped her up into his arms. "I don't think Melanie wants to hear about the horse right now. Maybe later."

When Melanie looked up into Zack's eyes, she realized he'd taken in the whole scene and come to a conclusion of his own.

Quickly she motioned to the present on the coffee table. "Jordan gave me a gift that made me a little weepy. I get like that at holidays." It was the only explanation she could come up with.

"Sorry we barged in like that," Zack muttered with a perturbed glance at Jordan. "I didn't know you intended to have company while we were gone." There was a cold note in his voice as if she'd planned this behind his back.

"I didn't know Jordan was coming."

With the tension getting worse, Jordan stood. "I had some time on my hands and decided to take a drive up here. But now I'd better be going."

"You don't have to leave on my account," Zack said. "Amy's going to take a nap, and I'm headed for my office. Feel free to stay as long as you want."

"I have patients to see when I get back."

Feeling awkward because Zack had seen her in Jordan's arms, Melanie turned to Amy. "I want to hear all about the horsey. After your nap you can draw me pictures of him.''

"No nap," Amy insisted. "Daw horsey." Then Amy reached her arms out to Melanie.

"I can take her back to her room," Zack insisted.

But Melanie took Amy from his arms. "No need for that. She can help me walk Jordan to the elevator."

Zack examined Amy's hold on Melanie's neck. "All right. Bring her to my office when you've finished and we'll decide about that nap." He strode down the hall.

Amy tucked her head into the crook of Melanie's shoulder, and she smoothed the little girl's hair back. "Are you sure you have to leave already, Jordan? Zack's offices are almost finished. I can give you a tour."

He shook his head. "I really do have to get back."

They crossed to the foyer and went out the door. At the elevator Jordan nodded to Amy. "I think she's the one who's going to help you get through the holidays."

"I think you're right about that," Melanie said softly. Then, holding Amy in one arm, she gave Jordan another hug with the other. "Thank you so much for the present. It's perfect."

At that he just gave her one of those Jordan smiles, stepped into the elevator and was gone.

"Bye-bye," Amy said as the doors closed.

Melanie bent her head against the little girl's. "Come on. Let's see if we can go talk your daddy out of that nap."

Chapter Nine

Still smarting from seeing Melanie in Jordan Wilson's arms, Zack pushed papers around his desk in his penthouse office on Monday afternoon.

Just friends, she'd said.

Had she ever kissed Jordan Wilson the way she'd kissed *him?*

Zack would bet his new headquarters that Jordan Wilson had known everything that had gone on in Melanie's life before now.

The door to Zack's office opened, and Ted Morgan peeked around the open door. "Flo said you were in here. Got a few minutes?"

Whenever his dad stopped in, he expected Zack to drop everything. Patiently Zack responded, "Sure, Pop. What's up?"

Ted came in and sat in front of Zack's desk. His flannel shirt was threadbare at the cuffs, and there was a hole in one elbow. Zack knew his dad had new shirts in his drawer but preferred his comfortable ones.

"I just wanted to check with you before I went out and bought Amy a few Christmas presents," Ted explained. "I found this little store with handmade wooden toys. They've got a dollhouse as big as she is. What do you think?"

Zack knew anything like that would be expensive and more than his dad should spend. "I'm not sure she'll be ready for a dollhouse until another year or two."

Ted looked disappointed. "I thought it was something she could keep to remember me by. But I do want to get her something she'd like. What are you buying her?"

His father had taken him completely off guard. He hadn't given much thought to Christmas, and it was time he did...for Amy's sake. "I'm not sure—puzzles, a doll, maybe another stuffed toy."

An awkward silence fell between them and, as in the past, Zack filled it with action. "How'd you like a tour of the offices? The rest of the furniture will be moved in this week. Melanie's supervising the installation of the drapes and blinds."

"I'd like to see what you're doing here."

Zack took his father on a tour beginning with the fourth floor. Ted didn't say much as they went from room to room, and Zack wondered if he was bored. They ran into Melanie on the first floor where computers still sat around in boxes. Up on a stepladder, she was fooling with a valance above the draperies.

Zack went over to her. "What are you doing? The installers should have done that."

"It's not hanging quite right." She looked over his shoulder at his father. "Hi, Ted."

Ted looked around at the striped teal draperies and

camel leather chairs, noticed the warm hues of the parquet flooring and the rich mahogany furniture, from the credenza to the computer desk. "You've done a wonderful job with this building, Melanie. It was a big project to get done in a short amount of time. All of it looks great."

A simmering anger came to the surface in Zack, not because his father was praising Melanie's accomplishments. She'd done a stupendous job with the offices. But just once Zack wished his father could realize that his son had accomplished something, too.

Melanie's gaze locked on Zack's. "Did you show your dad the sculpture downstairs?"

"We didn't tour the lobby yet," Zack said gruffly.

Ted glanced from one of them to the other. "Why don't you help her with whatever's wrong with those drapes, and I'll go take a look around myself. Can I get out through the lobby?"

"Yes, you can," she answered him. "There's a guard on duty down there now."

"I'll introduce myself. Then he'll know who I am and won't give me any hassles when I want to come up."

Melanie was about to step off the ladder when Zack went over to her and held her elbow, making sure she kept her balance. They hadn't touched since Saturday night when they'd almost— The remembered pleasure made his body tighten. They hadn't even had a decent conversation. But now wasn't the time to ask her what that scene with Wilson had been all about.

"Wait a minute, Pop," he tossed over his shoulder. To Melanie he said, "If you need help with anything else like this, have one of the workmen help you, or call me. I don't want you falling off the ladder."

Then he turned back to his father. "I'll walk you down and introduce you to the guard myself."

After he escorted his dad to the stairway, they started down the inside steps.

"Are you getting anywhere with her?" Ted asked Zack as soon as the fire door closed behind them.

Zack tried to keep his temper in check. "Just what do you mean by 'getting anywhere'?"

"Have you asked her to stay past when her job's done?"

"Why would I do that?"

"Because you like her...because she's just the kind of woman you need," Ted answered with a wave of his hand that said Zack should realize the obvious.

"How do you know what kind of woman I need? You think every man needs someone like Mom. Women aren't like that anymore." Attempting to close the discussion, Zack started down the stairs.

Ted caught his arm. "If you can't see that Melanie *is* like your mother, then you're blind, boy."

After a few heavy, silent moments, Zack pulled away, and they descended the rest of the stairs.

When they entered the lobby, its sense of executive luxuriance overtook Zack once more. The imported Mexican tile floor was instantly welcoming in a professional way. The swirled plaster walls with the palest tint of sky blue rose into the vaulted ceiling where daylight streamed in through a skylight. A bronze plaque had gone up inside the glass doors as a directory to the departments. Seating areas in camel leather and oak made waiting seem a pleasure while potted palms added year-round freshness. On an oak dais in the center of the lobby stood the sculpture Zack had chosen.

After looking around at everything else, Ted went to

it, then whistled through his teeth. "Isn't that something? And just right for in here. Melanie sure does have good taste."

"*I* chose it," Zack said evenly. "And you know, Pop, Melanie *did* do an excellent job. But just once it would be nice to hear that I did, too…that these headquarters are a symbol of what I've accomplished and maybe how proud you are of that."

Ted looked astonished. "I've always been proud of everything you do. I didn't think I had to say it."

Zack searched his dad's face for the truth. "I've never known you were proud of what I've accomplished. I've always had the feeling I can't please you. You wanted me to go to college instead of business school. You wanted me to be a banker, not fool around with sports equipment. How am I supposed to know what you think about me and what I do?"

"*You* never want to talk about anything you do," Ted insisted. "You act as though I don't understand it. I understand a lot more than you think. I understand that you've never forgiven me because I took your mom to the hospital and you never saw her again. I understand that you think I did it on purpose. I understand that you were ashamed of me because I didn't wear a suit or drive one of those fancy cars like some of your friends' fathers did."

"I've never been ashamed of you, Pop!"

"Never?"

Zack tried to be honest and realized that he and his dad had never really talked after his mother died, had never really shared anything. But they couldn't get into all of that now. Not here. He strove to make the conversation less serious. "There is that one time you came to my Halloween party as a scarecrow. You looked pitiful.''

Ted's head shot up, and then he realized Zack was kidding. ''That's the only time?''

''Look, Pop. I don't know why you walk around with frayed shirt cuffs and holes in your sleeves. But if that's the way you want to live, and that's what makes you happy, that's fine with me.''

Heavy silence became a wall between them until Ted asked, ''And what about your mother?''

Maybe they couldn't postpone this discussion any longer...maybe they'd postponed it too long already. Searching his heart, Zack knew he'd never hated his dad. He'd been angry. But what good had that anger done him except driven a wedge between him and the person who missed his mother as much as he did?

''I don't hate you,'' he said hoarsely. ''I felt you did keep me from Mom on purpose, that you wanted those last few minutes with her rather than share her with me,'' he admitted honestly. ''I've been angry about it for so long I don't know what it's like not to be angry.''

''It wasn't like that,'' Ted denied vehemently. ''Everything happened so fast, Zack. Lord almighty, I never expected it to happen that fast. If I had known, I would have pulled you out of school. Honest to goodness, I would have.''

Zack felt his throat tighten, and his heart ached for all the time that he and his dad had seemed to be at odds. They weren't really. They were from two generations. Yet that didn't mean they couldn't have a meeting of the minds now and then...or remember together.

Ted awkwardly cleared his throat, not knowing how to go on with this kind of conversation, since they'd never attempted to share pent-up feelings before. He motioned to the sculpture. "So you picked this out, huh? You've got taste."

"Melanie introduced the artist's work to me. She's got taste, too. And you were right. She *is* like Mom in lots of ways." He knew they were both thinking *and very different from Sherry.*

But he didn't want to get into that, too. Thinking about the conversation he and his dad had had earlier in his office, he made a decision. "Since I haven't bought Amy her Christmas presents yet, and since you don't know what to get her, why don't we go shopping together later this week? Then maybe we can stop in one of those sports bars for a beer."

Ted looked as if Zack had just handed him all his Christmas presents in one fell swoop. "I'd like that. I'd like it a lot." His voice had grown a bit husky and he cleared his throat again. "Well, I'd better let you get back to work. You want to call me on what night suits you best?"

"I'll do that."

When Ted exited the glass lobby doors, Zack realized he'd never introduced him to the guard. Ted gave a last wave goodbye as he left the building. Zack knew there would be plenty more opportunities to do it because he and his dad had finally seemed to find some common ground.

It was almost five o'clock as Melanie made a check of the second- third- and fourth-floor window treatments. All of them were perfect, exactly what she'd ordered. Yet she felt an odd restlessness that had been with her all day. Instead of taking the private elevator up to the penthouse, she walked down four flights of steps, went into the lobby and stood looking at the statue. She still hadn't gone into Santa Rosa to buy herself a heavier jacket. Actually she needed a ski outfit to take along to Winter Haven. But just the thought of setting foot in the stores with the bright twinkling multicolored lights, the tinsel garlands and wreaths made her dismiss the idea until it was absolutely necessary. She'd been thinking about Phil and Kaitlyn all day. Tomorrow was the eighteenth of December. It was a day she'd rather skip, a day that would bring pain with every tick of the clock's hand.

You can get through it, she told herself as she gazed at the sculpture Vincente Largo had created. She would spend tomorrow checking inventory lists, rearranging furniture, making sure nothing was missing and everything was in its place. There'd be more delivery men coming, and she could start early and work very late.

Needing to take a few deep, calming breaths to stay emotions that were on the verge of going on a rampage, she waved to the guard. "I'll see you tomorrow, Harry."

"Sure will, Miss Carlotti. You have a good evening." Harry was in his fifties and had retired from the Santa Rosa police force two years ago. At his wife's urging he'd gone into private security work because life was too short to take any more risks. He was pleasant and friendly and guarded Zack's headquarters as if they were Fort Knox.

Thinking about Harry relieved some of her tension as Melanie went outside and looked up at the sky. The stars were as white as ice and the moon was a golden crescent. A breeze swept by her, though, and she shivered in her light coat. Usually she couldn't wait to get upstairs to see Amy, help Flo get dinner on the table and wait for Zack. But tonight…

Tonight she was too full of memories, too ready to wallow in self-pity that wouldn't do her any good, too close to giving in to grief she thought she'd put behind her. As she walked around to the penthouse's outside entrance, she knew she was being a coward. It was time to go upstairs, look at Jordan's plaque and put everything in perspective.

Still, perspective didn't come easily on a night like this.

Instead of buzzing Flo, she used the key Zack had given her to open the outside entrance and let herself into the hallway. When the door locked behind her, she had the eerie feeling she wouldn't be able to escape from everything that had happened in the past or the reason why she'd come here. She stepped into the elevator and, as it rose to the penthouse, she thought about the upcoming holiday and the ski trip, as well as the grand opening of Zack's headquarters.

Then what?

When she let herself into the penthouse, she smelled the wonderful aromas of vanilla and cookie dough. In the kitchen, she saw Flo frosting cookies with colored icing and Amy sitting in her high chair nibbling on a star with red sparkles.

Melanie's heart ached so badly she could hardly catch her breath. She'd decorated this same kind of cookie with Kaitlyn. She remembered blue and pink and yellow icing all over her daughter's face, on her fingers, in her hair. Tears pricked in Melanie's eyes and she fought to blink them away.

Attempting a lightness she didn't feel, she shrugged out of her coat. "That's some supper you have there."

Amy grinned at her. "Cookie."

Flo laughed. "Don't you believe her. That cookie is her dessert. Zack told me he wouldn't be here for supper—he had to run some errands. I fed Amy early so I could get started on these. There's barbecued beef in the Crock-Pot and salad in the refrigerator."

"I had a late lunch," Melanie said quickly, needing to get away from the aromas and Flo's smile and Amy's sweetness. "I'll get something la—"

There was a ruckus in the foyer, a rustle, a thump, and then Zack called, "Come here, everyone. See what I've got."

By the time Flo scooped Amy from her high chair and followed Melanie into the hall, Zack had moved into the living room. When Melanie stepped into the archway, she saw him in the corner by the sofa, proudly motioning to an eight-foot-high and very full Christmas tree.

"What do you think?" he asked as the smell of pine filled the air.

Every picture of Christmas that Melanie had stored in her memory seemed to explode in her mind. She saw the first Christmas tree she and Phil had decorated together, followed by images of Kaitlyn as a baby staring mesmerized at colored lights on the tree. The bare fir in Zack's living room became an evergreen adorned with old-fashioned, large frosted-ball lights that had decorated Phil's parents' tree when they were alive. He'd insisted they were safe. He'd insisted they'd only light them for an hour at a time. The night of the fire, he'd gone to bed early and left them plugged in.

She'd lost her child because of those lights. She'd lost everything...

That night two years ago filled her head and made

her heart race. She didn't hear or see Zack approach because she was miles, and two Christmases ago, away. She'd been sipping eggnog when a passerby had alerted everyone at Barbara's party that smoke was seeping out under the eaves of Melanie's house. At first she couldn't believe it. Then she'd heard a distant siren. Panicked, she'd run from Barbara's house to her own. Desperate to get to her daughter, she'd opened the door. The night had burst into smoke…and flame…and shattered glass.

"Melanie, what's wrong?" Zack was standing at her elbow, his expression worried.

She was shaking all over and couldn't stop it. She was barely aware of him saying to Flo, "Take Amy back to the kitchen." Then he was tugging Melanie toward the sofa where she almost fell because her knees were so weak.

He lowered himself beside her, his arm around her, holding her close. "Tell me, Melanie. Tell me what's happening to you."

Covering her face with her hands, she shook and let the tears come, more tears than she'd cried in months and months and months. As the tears flowed, her trembling became less violent, the memories less vivid, though the aching in her heart was sharp and deep and as alive as it had been after she had awakened in the hospital, her eyes patched, her family gone.

Still Zack held her, his strength leading her back to the here and now…her love for him bringing her to her moment of truth. She had to tell him about everything. She had to do it now.

Finally she wiped the tears from her face and turned to look at him.

"Tell me what happened to you," Zack demanded gently.

Closing her eyes, she took a bolstering breath. "I...I had a daughter. She was four and—" Melanie's voice caught. "Her name was Kaitlyn. She was the most beautiful little girl—blond hair, blue eyes, perfect in every way. Like Amy." She swallowed hard, knowing she had to do this, yet dreading the telling, dreading Zack's response. "My husband, Phil..." She cleared her throat. "He was a lovable man, but he was often irresponsible. I didn't trust him with Kaitlyn completely. He didn't watch her closely enough. He spent money like water so I took charge of the finances. But we loved each other and our marriage worked. Still, I often felt I had two children rather than one."

"What happened the night of the fire?" Zack asked, prodding her.

Melanie's gaze collided with his. "You know?"

"I overheard your conversation with Tom Kellison. You wouldn't tell me anything about what had happened to you, so the next day I went to the newspaper archives in Santa Rosa. I found the article about the fire."

Her voice was a hoarse whisper. "You didn't say anything."

"I wanted you to tell me yourself. I wanted you to trust me enough to confide in me."

Now she was confiding in him. But he didn't realize how much he was a part of all of it, too. "When I saw the Christmas tree you brought in, everything came flooding back because...our tree lights caused the fire. Our neighbor had a party around four. It was going to stretch long into the evening. Phil was a systems manager and he'd been on call the night before. He hadn't gotten home until around nine in the morning, but he'd stayed up to play with Kaitlyn—so we could all spend the day together. I wasn't going to go to the party," she remembered, her voice low. "But Barbara was a good friend. Phil encouraged me to go, saying he'd put Kaitlyn to bed early and he'd go to bed, too."

"He left on the Christmas tree lights?" Zack asked.

Melanie's lower lip trembled. "The lights were older ones—like frosted balls. I warned him they gave off too much heat, but he said we'd watch them, we wouldn't leave them on for long periods of time unless we were in the room. But he must have forgotten to unplug them."

Zack's arm was still around her, and she wished he would keep it there forever. "Someone walking down the street saw smoke seeping out under the eaves of our house. They had a cell phone and called 911, then came to Barbara's to alert us since our house was next door to hers. I didn't stop to think about anything but getting to Kaitlyn. I ran over there and pulled open the door... There was an explosion."

"Backdraft," Zack said. "Oxygen feeding the fire."

Melanie nodded, seeing the smoke again, reliving the panic, the moment she pulled open the door... "The windows shattered and I was knocked off the porch. I was unconscious until I woke up in the hospital and found out—" She stopped now to take a deep breath because Sherry Morgan's part of the story started here. "My eyes were bandaged. The shattered glass had damaged the corneas and if I was ever going to see again, I needed corneal transplants in both eyes."

"Oh, my God, Melanie." He took her face between his hands. "What an unbelievable amount of loss. How did you survive it?"

His hands on her face were comforting...so welcome. ''I prayed and relied on faith I'd had since I was a child. Jordan was my ophthalmologist and he was very supportive.''

Zack's fingers brushed lightly down her cheeks as he leaned away then, studying her. ''Obviously the transplant procedure was a success.''

''Yes, it was. But it took about nine months until my eyes healed enough so I could have the procedure. It was hard to cope. My friend Barbara invited me to stay with her and her family. I don't know what I would have done without them. I couldn't see and they were so patient with me, so helpful without treating me like an invalid. Even after the operation it took a long time to get my sight back.''

''But you did.''

''Yes.'' Then she said the words that had to be said, the words that would change everything. ''I got my sight back because of your wife.''

Her statement reverberated in the room until Zack broke the heavy silence. ''Sherry was an organ donor.''

''Yes.'' She wished she could leave it at that. She wished she could just tell him she'd come to thank him...to thank Sherry in a way. Yet she couldn't. She had to be completely honest with him. ''It's a bit more complicated than that, though.''

She couldn't read Zack's expression when he asked neutrally, ''Aren't the files of organ donors and recipients kept confidential?''

''Yes. And I never would have tried to find the donor except I *had* to.''

Now he shifted away from her. ''Why did you have to?''

How could she explain this so he'd understand? *She*

still didn't understand. So she simply related what had happened. "Immediately after surgery I began having dreams. I heard a woman's voice, but I couldn't understand what she was saying to me. And there was always a man in the dreams." She paused and then went on, "That man was you."

Now he was staring at her as if she had lost her mind in the explosion, too. "How could I be in your dreams when you'd never met me?"

"I didn't know. I didn't know who you were. I didn't understand what was happening. But the dreams kept recurring, and I had these feelings and yearnings that I didn't understand, either. They didn't feel like mine."

His eyes narrowed and his brow creased. "This sounds like some sort of plot for a grade B movie."

"It was no movie, Zack," she quietly assured him. "I couldn't sleep at night, was upset during the day. I had my eyesight back but I wasn't at peace. I had to find out what it was all about. So I hired a private investigator and he found out Sherry was my donor. He gave me information about you, too. That's how I knew you needed an interior decorator. Through it all, it seemed as if someone was leading me…as if I were on a mission."

"A mission to do what?" he exploded.

"I don't know. I'm still not sure. But when I met you I knew you were the man I'd seen in my dreams."

Now he was shaking his head with disbelief. "How do you expect me to believe any of this?"

"Because I'm telling you it's so."

With the certainty in her voice, his gaze met hers and he studied her for long moments. Wariness replaced his disbelief. "You came here under false pretenses to do what? Replace the family you'd lost?"

Her throat tightened again, but she managed, "Nothing can replace the family I lost. And I didn't come here under false pretenses. You needed a decorator."

"Not one with ulterior motives. What do you want from me?"

How intricately complicated that question was. "I believe I was led here, Zack. By Sherry. I don't know why. Maybe because I can give you and Amy something you need."

"Oh, you can give me something I need, all right." His eyes raked her from her tear-stained face to her flat shoes. "You've almost proved that more than once. But after this cockamamie story you've told me..." His voice had gone cold, his eyes hard.

She protested, "It's the truth!"

"It's the truth according to *you*. I believed who you said you were. Now I don't know what you are, and to think I let you get close to my daughter—"

Hurt, she slid away from him...from his disbelief. "I would *never* hurt Amy. I've come to care for her...deeply. I care about you, too. Don't you see this wasn't just some whim of mine? The dreams—"

He raked his hand through his hair. "Dreams mean nothing. As far as you believing I was in them... You probably saw a shadow and then when you saw *me,* you wanted to believe I was the man in your dreams. This is real life, Melanie, but I don't think you have a good grip on it."

The way Zack was looking at her made tears come to her eyes again. They welled up, and before they spilled over she looked away. This was too much for Zack to absorb at one time, too much to absorb with her here. "I understand that this is a lot for you to take in, and I know it must all sound fantastic. But I came here because I felt there was something Sherry wanted me to tell you. I still don't know what that is. Whatever it is, maybe you can help me figure it out.''

At that, Zack's face became even stonier, and she knew he wasn't in the mood to listen to any more tonight…maybe not anytime soon. She made a decision. ''I think it would be better if I leave. I can stay at the motel in Cool Ridge and then look for a place in Santa Rosa over the weekend.''

Silent, he stared out the huge picture window into the night as if searching for the truth about her. When he didn't respond, she stood and went to her bedroom.

Tears were too close to the surface tonight, and Melanie did her best to keep them at bay as she pulled her suitcase from her closet and laid it on the bed. She was methodically filling it with the clothes in the dresser drawers when Amy came toddling in, moving much faster than usual. Melanie was afraid Amy was running so fast she'd fall.

The little girl came over to her and wrapped her arms around Melanie's legs. ''Mellie, Mellie. Cookies. Nighty-night.''

Amy wanted Melanie to put her to bed, that was obvious. Tears openly flowing now, she didn't know what to do.

When Zack followed Amy into Melanie's room, he stopped in his tracks. Melanie's tears and what she'd been through tore at him. He watched as she picked up Amy and held the little girl as if she were the most precious child in the world. He didn't know what to think of her wild story and her motives, but it was obvious she cared for his daughter. Spending Christmas with Amy could give her back some of what she'd lost with her own child.

But what if she was crazy?

He took a deep breath. After practically living with her all these weeks, he knew she wasn't crazy. Misguided maybe. On a mission that might have nothing to do with him but rather with her own loss. After everything she'd done for him and Amy and his offices, he couldn't deprive her of spending Christmas with his daughter.

Crossing to them, he said, "It'll be a little difficult to put out cookies and milk for Santa if you're in Cool Ridge or Santa Rosa. Besides, you've a lot of work to do to get ready for the grand opening. It would be inconvenient for you to find your own place before then."

At his words there was so much hope in Melanie's eyes he had to dispel it. "I don't believe your dreams are anything more than your way of coping with loss. As long as we're clear on that, there's no reason why you can't finish my project, is there?"

She hesitated only a moment, "No. No reason. But Zack—the ski trip. Do you want me to stay here while you go?"

"That trip is your Christmas bonus, Melanie. I don't renege. You'll have your own chalet. There's no reason why we can't ski and enjoy a few days away."

"I was afraid to tell you all of this when I first came."

With good reason, he thought. "If you had, I wouldn't have given you the job."

Then he took Amy from Melanie's arms. "Let's go see if we have anything to use to decorate that Christmas tree."

When he left Melanie's room with his daughter, he was more unsettled than he'd ever been in his life.

Chapter Ten

Ten days later Melanie waited for Zack at the top of the ski run, knowing her time with him was running out, and not knowing what to do about it. He still looked at her with the same intensity. Chemistry still sparkled between them. But there was a wariness in him now. He'd kept his distance since the night she'd told him everything, and she hadn't mentioned her dreams again. He thought they were a product of the trauma she'd gone through, and she supposed that was better than having him think she was crazy.

They'd spent Christmas together, with Flo and Amy acting as buffers. Ted had come over and had given her odd looks, as if he'd known something was wrong. Yet he hadn't asked her, and she didn't know if he'd mentioned the obvious tension to Zack. He and his dad seemed more comfortable with each other now. She didn't know what had caused the change, but she was glad of it. Any and all bonds were precious. She knew they could be severed from one day to the next.

Now as Zack joined her again at the top of the intermediate ski run, she admired how gracefully he moved on his skis, how handsome and strong and athletic he looked in his black ski suit with its jagged yellow streak on the sleeves. Though he was an expert skier, they'd spent the morning on the milder slopes, and she'd gotten her confidence back. Zack had told her he'd skied this run often over the years and it matched her level of skill. She suspected it was easy for him.

As he skied toward her, she thought about last night as she'd sat in her chalet alone…and gone to bed alone. She'd prayed for a miracle. Not an open-the-sky-and-see-an-angel kind of miracle, but just something—something that would make Zack realize what they had between them, something that would make him realize he could move on, something that would encourage him to believe in her and what she felt.

As he stopped beside her, ski poles poised, he gave her one of those friendly smiles that didn't reach his eyes. "Ready?"

She nodded, letting him take the lead as she had all morning, letting him show her the way.

The sun had slipped behind a cloud, and as Melanie concentrated on the downward slope before her, she caught a glimpse of Zack approaching a stand of pines. Suddenly, like a movie playing in front of her eyes, she knew right before he swerved away from the trees that his skis would skid on a patch of unseen ice and he'd forcefully slam into one of those pines. She couldn't let that happen.

Picking up speed, she called after him, "Zack! Zack, stop! There's ice over there. You'll hit it and run into the tree."

She didn't know if he'd heard what she said, but he slid to a sudden stop about twenty yards from the pines and waited until she caught up. "What did you say?"

This knowing or vision was like her dreams—insubstantial, seemingly fantastic. Still, she knew what she'd felt and "seen." She pointed to an area by the trees. "Over there. There's ice. I saw you hitting it and running into the tree."

Pushing his goggles on top of his head, he just stared at her, stunned.

"Zack, I know you said not to tell you anything else. I know this doesn't seem real. But I saw it happening. I couldn't let you just—"

"It *did* happen," he said gruffly.

His words caught her by surprise. "What?"

"It *did* happen. Three years ago. I slid, ran into that tree, and broke my leg. You've got to tell me the truth about this, Melanie. Did you find out about that? Did Pop tell you? Your private investigator?"

"*No one* told me. I saw it happening. I didn't realize it was in the past. I didn't realize it was Sherry's memory…until now."

His cheeks had been ruddy from the sun and the wind, but now he looked ashen, shell-shocked, as if his world had been shaken to its core. She knew that feeling well.

"Zack, I know you don't want to hear it, but I've had Sherry's memories before. When we went to San Francisco, behind the restaurant, remember? You told me that was the last place you and Sherry had been happy. That wasn't true. She was always happy with you. She just wanted you to realize how much her career meant to her."

"Melanie, stop."

"I can't, Zack. You have to know. Then that day at your dad's with the Christmas lights. Sherry knew you put blue lights in the middle and white on the sides. I didn't. It just came out before I even thought about it. Don't you see? There's something you need to settle, something you're not at peace about because she isn't, either."

As the cold wind swept by them, his words seemed even colder. "You don't know what the hell you're talking about."

His attitude was breaking her heart. "No, I don't. But I think you do. If you just talk to me about it—"

"Talk to you about what?" he cut in. "Talk to you as if you were my wife? I don't think so. I can't believe something so bizarre, and I'm still not sure any of it's true. Maybe it's just one big hoax you're trying to pull."

His accusation lanced deeper than anything he'd said before when he'd simply thought she was misguided. "Why would I do that?" she managed.

"I don't know. That's what I have to try to figure out. Let's finish this run and get back to the chalet." Then he pushed his ski poles into the snow and took off—away from her and everything he didn't want to face.

The day after Melanie returned with Zack and Amy and Flo from the ski vacation, she checked Zack's headquarters to make sure everything was the way it was supposed to be. The last of the furniture had been moved in.

Since they'd returned from Winter Haven, Zack had hardly spoken to her. Every time their gazes met, she knew what he thought of her. Last night it had hurt so much she'd decided to move out of the penthouse as soon as possible. If she couldn't find an apartment today, she'd move to a motel.

Her mind was spinning as she drove to Santa Rosa—the Apartment for Rent page of the newspaper beside her. The day was as gray as her emotions. She and Zack had hardly seen each other the last two days of their vacation. He'd come in from the slopes yesterday while she was playing with Amy and had barely been civil. He obviously believed she had some grand scheme up her sleeve, that she wanted to marry him to replace the family she'd lost or maybe simply marry him because he was well-to-do. She didn't know how to convince him otherwise, and the best thing for all of them was for her to move out.

Over the next two hours as she examined apartments, she realized she hadn't yet decorated the penthouse for Zack. It was just as well. He wouldn't want reminders of her anywhere around.

The third apartment she looked at she liked. It was even available immediately if she wanted it. The tenant had moved out before the holidays, and management had had it cleaned. It was in immaculate condition. Melanie knew it was best if she took it today. She wrote out a check and gave it to the manager.

Fifteen minutes later she drove through Santa Rosa, still preoccupied with Zack and Amy and everything she'd be leaving. She couldn't stem the flow of tears again. She'd cried more in the past two weeks than she had after the fire. Had all of this been for nothing? She couldn't believe that. She couldn't let it end like this. Sherry Morgan wanted something from her, and Zack needed whatever it was.

Instead of taking the road that led to Cool Ridge and

Zack's headquarters, Melanie turned down a main street and then a series of side streets heading for Ted Morgan's house. She had an idea and maybe he could help her.

The sky had become even grayer by the time Ted answered his door. He took one look at her face and ushered her inside. "What's going on, Melanie?"

"It's very complicated, but I need the answers to some questions and I thought you could help. Zack won't."

"All right. Shoot."

"Do you know what happened the night of Sherry's accident?"

After a considering moment, Ted shook his head. "No. Zack never talks about it."

Melanie felt stalled before she got started, but one way or another, she was going to find out what had happened. "Can you tell me where it happened?"

Looking puzzled, Ted asked, "Why do you want to know?"

"Just tell me, Ted, please."

"From what I understand, it happened on a road outside of Cool Ridge. It's a shortcut to Zack's new headquarters. He was in the site trailer, working late."

"Tell me *exactly* where it happened."

Seeing her determination, Ted gave her a few landmarks.

"Thanks, Ted." She went to the door.

"That's it? You're not going to stay and have a cup of tea with me?" He seemed concerned, and she wished she could tell him not to be.

"No tea today. There are a few things I have to do. Maybe another time."

Then she left before the compassion in Ted Morgan's

eyes made her spill the whole story and she'd have to face his judgment of her motives, too.

In her car forty-five minutes later, Melanie took the road Ted had told her about—an alternate route that would lead her to Zack's headquarters. It was narrower than the two-lane road that ran through Cool Ridge. It was also bumpier and curvier. As she drove Melanie was absolutely aware that this was the way Sherry had traveled that fateful night. Melanie tried not to let her anxiety and helplessness over the situation with Zack overtake her. She tried to clear her mind and her heart so she could feel—feel not only her own feelings, but Sherry's, too.

A drizzling rain began to fall, and Melanie turned on her windshield wipers, keeping her eyes peeled for a small gas station Ted had described as a landmark. She passed a red-and-blue house trailer and then a cedar-sided, ranch-style home. The curve Ted had also described was right beyond the house. That was where the accident had happened.

On alert, Melanie spotted the sharp curve, the ditch along the road, the live oaks bordering it. Slowing to a stop, she knew she couldn't park along the curve, so she backed up a safe distance, almost in front of the house, hoping whoever was inside wouldn't mind. There was a feeling stirring in her chest, the flash of a picture in her mind of a dark green sedan tilted into that ditch, its front end smashed into the trees. She really didn't care about the rain as she exited her car and walked toward that ditch. It drew her like an unbearably strong magnet.

The falling rain was icy as it pelted her face and wet her hair. That didn't seem to matter. There was something here she had to see...had to know...had to do.

She didn't know how long she walked in and out of the trees and along the ditch, but suddenly she heard someone call, "Hello, there," and she looked up.

An elderly lady with a wrinkled, weathered face, her hair in a bun on top of her head, a plastic rain bonnet tied under her chin, walked toward her using a cane. She was a bit stooped over, and her silvery raincoat almost fell to her ankles.

When she was a few feet from Melanie, Melanie apologized. "I'm sorry if I'm trespassing."

The woman waved one feeble hand at her. "That's all right. I don't get many visitors. Are you lost?"

"Not exactly. My name's Melanie," she said introducing herself.

"Beatrice Martin," the woman responded, extending her hand. "Everyone calls me Bea."

Melanie shook the woman's hand, and although it was thin and fragile, there was strength in it.

"So what brings you out here?" Bea asked. "I saw you through the window. Are you looking for something?"

"Yes, I am. But I'm not sure what. Someone I know had an accident out here. It happened over a year ago. A green sedan went off the road into this tree."

"Oh, I remember that one. The driver was going pretty fast."

I forgot about the curve, Melanie heard in her head. *It was lightning and thundering…getting dark…and my windshield wipers couldn't keep up with the rain.*

Melanie's breath caught as she listened to the voice inside her head…to the voice inside her heart. She swallowed hard. "Mrs. Martin…"

"Bea," the woman reminded her.

"Bea," Melanie repeated with a shaky smile. "Was it almost dark?"

"Sure was. Terrible storm, too. I heard the car and then I heard the smash-up. Awful it was. I called 911. I knew there was nothing I could do. The ambulance got here pretty fast."

But it was too late, Sherry's voice told her. *Too late to tell Zack...*

Melanie waited for the rest, but it didn't come.

"After the ambulance left," Bea went on, "the tow truck took the car away." She cocked her head and stared at Melanie. "I found something the next day. It must have fallen out of the car when they towed it away."

Melanie's heart pounded. "What did you find?"

"I'll go get it. It didn't seem right to throw it away. But I didn't know what to do with it. Come with me. You can have a cup of tea and get out of this rain."

As Melanie walked beside the older lady toward her house, she heard a car coming around the curve. As it slowed, pulled off the road and parked in front of hers, she recognized it. It was Zack's. Ted must have called him. How was she going to explain this? Coming here, searching for...

Whatever this lady had in her house was very important.

She'd reached Bea's front stoop when Zack came striding toward her, looking angry. He was wearing a blue flannel shirt and jeans and hadn't even bothered with a coat.

"What are you doing here?" he demanded when he reached her.

"I had to follow my instincts. I had to follow Sherry's voice."

"For God's sake, Melanie! Why can't you let it alone?"

Bea returned outside then and handed Melanie the white plastic satchel with the department store's name written on the front. "Here's what I found."

Melanie's hands trembled as she took the package from Bea, opened the bag and slid out a pair of variegated pink-and-blue baby booties. The booties in her dreams. She held them out to Zack. "These mean something, Zack. They were in Sherry's car and fell out when the car was towed away."

The tortured look in his eyes made her wish she wasn't doing this to him. But then in a flash of insight, with Sherry's voice clear in her head, she understood why she'd been led here...why she'd had to find Zack. As he reached out for the booties, she knew clearly why Sherry had led her to him and what all of it meant.

Bea looked from one of them to the other, mumbled an excuse and stepped back into the house. The storm door clicked shut. Rain drizzled down on Zack and Melanie as Zack stared at the booties.

"Sherry changed her mind," Melanie said breathlessly. "She'd accepted being pregnant because she loved you. She bought these for the new baby as a sign she wanted the child as much as you did. She was driving up here to tell you that."

Zack gazed at the booties, heard Melanie's words and then raised his head to look at her. He felt as if his life was spinning around him—as if the past had caught up to the present. His dad had called him, worried about Melanie. His father had told Zack where she was going. Rattled by Melanie's wild proclamation on the mountain, the idea of her hearing Sherry's voice and having

Sherry's memories, he'd driven out here furious with Melanie, yet torn by other feelings, too.

Now as he gazed into her blue eyes, he realized what she was saying was true. He realized somehow she *could* hear Sherry's voice...or her thoughts. And he finally understood what it all meant. Sherry didn't wreck the car on purpose or try to lose the baby. She was looking forward to their life together and had accepted the idea of another child. Her accident had been simply that—an accident.

Emotion choked him, and he couldn't speak. He could only rub his fingers over the baby booties as the wash of relief, but also grief over everything he'd lost, lapped over him.

Melanie must have seen it. Her own eyes filled with tears. "I'm sorry, Zack. I'm sorry you lost Sherry and your unborn child."

He couldn't respond to her. He couldn't make sense of everything roiling inside him.

"I—I've got to get back to the penthouse," Melanie murmured. "Out of the rain...out of your life." The last was a whisper as she took off across the yard to her car. She had climbed in and had pulled onto the road, headed back to the penthouse, before what she'd said had sunk in.

Out of his life? What did she mean by that? He didn't want her out of his life. He...

So many realizations battered him at once. He loved Melanie Carlotti. He'd been fighting it for weeks. He'd been guarding himself against it because of the guilt he still felt about Sherry's accident, about their argument, about the way he felt about her because she hadn't wanted his child. But now he could let go of all of it. Now he was free to really live again...to love again.

There was only one woman he wanted to love now, wanted to spend the rest of his life with, wanted as a mother for Amy.

Bea opened her door again then, and peeked out at him. "Mister, you want to come in out of the rain? I told Melanie I'd make her a cup of tea, but she ran off. I can make one for you."

"No. No tea, thanks. I have to catch Melanie." He rushed toward his car.

But he heard the little old lady say, "Drive carefully."

He waved a hand in acknowledgment and yanked open his door, still overwhelmed by everything that had happened, suddenly afraid Melanie wouldn't be able to forgive his doubts or the harsh things he'd said. He'd never known true fear before, but now he did. He couldn't let Melanie leave. He had to make her understand that he loved her.

When Zack rushed into the penthouse, Flo saw his expression. "What in heaven's name happened?"

"You won't believe it if I tell you," Zack muttered.

"Melanie ran in here, said she'd found an apartment in Santa Rosa. She's packing. She's leaving!"

"She can't leave."

"Well, she is. She went into her bedroom and shut the door. Amy's sitting outside of it. Melanie doesn't know she's there. I wasn't sure what to do."

"I'll take care of it," he called to Flo as he hurried down the hall.

His daughter sat outside of Melanie's door, holding on to BoBo for dear life. She looked up at him with big wide eyes.

"Mommy...Mellie." Amy didn't look confused or troubled but very certain.

It might be shorthand language, but Zack understood Amy perfectly, clearly saw the meaning of her words in her eyes. Melanie was a gift that Sherry had given to him and Amy. Melanie had been sent here to bring him peace and to make his life whole again. He hadn't been ready to accept the gift before, but now he was. It was as if Sherry had picked out Melanie for him, a perfect mate, one who had his values and sentiments and goals and dreams.

Scooping his daughter into his arms, he hugged her, and then he looked up to heaven. "Thank you," he murmured. To Amy he said, "I need to talk to Melanie alone this time, but you and Flo can get some hot chocolate and cookies ready. Okay?"

His daughter gazed into his eyes and then gave him a cherubic smile. "Okay," she agreed.

After Zack settled Amy in the kitchen with Flo, he went back to Melanie's room and knocked sharply on the door.

When she didn't answer, he turned the knob and went inside.

Once before she'd tried to pack to leave and he'd stopped her, telling himself it was because of her contract, because he needed her to finish supervising the opening of the headquarters, because he'd wanted to give her Christmas with his daughter. That time she'd packed neatly. Now she was just tossing clothes into the suitcase. Her hair was wet from the rain and there were tear streaks on her cheeks. He hoped he wasn't too late to make her believe they could have a future together.

"You can't leave," he said hoarsely.

She didn't look at him and she didn't stop moving. "I have to leave. You still love Sherry. Maybe you always will. I could see that when you realized what those booties meant."

"What you saw was overwhelming relief. I thought I had caused her accident. I thought maybe *she'd* caused it on purpose to lose the baby. She'd told me she didn't want to be pregnant again, that she'd wanted to terminate the pregnancy. I couldn't abide that idea. It was the worst argument we'd ever had."

Still Melanie didn't stop packing.

Frustrated now, he went to her and took her by the shoulders. "Melanie, you have to listen to me. I love you. I've been fighting that love for weeks. I don't begin to understand any of this…or anything about what happened to you…or what led you out to that accident site today. But I *do* know you were sent to me and not just as a messenger to tell me what Sherry couldn't tell me herself. You're a gift from her or from Someone who knows how much I need you in my life. You've given me perspective again. You make me want to smile and truly feel. I've been guarding myself against feeling for a very long time. I appreciate life so much more when I'm with you."

He took a deep breath and rushed on. "I know I doubted you. I know I said things you might not be able to forgive. But I love you, Melanie. Can you try to forgive my lack of faith? Will you marry me?"

She looked stunned.

His hands slid from her shoulders to her face. "I love you," he said again.

"Oh, Zack." She threw her arms around his neck and hugged him as if she never wanted to let him go.

He held her then, feeling so full of love and gratitude he had to swallow hard.

Eventually Melanie pulled away and gazed into his eyes. "I love you too, Zack. So much. And I love Amy. The longer I was with you and Amy, the more I could tell Sherry's feelings from mine. She just wanted you to be free."

"I see that now. I see how courageous you've been in not giving up on me. Can you forgive the way I doubted you?"

Her blue eyes shimmered with all of her feeling for him. "Yes, I can forgive you."

He couldn't keep from kissing her then, from bringing her so close that they were almost one. Their kiss was more than a declaration of love. It was a promise that they'd never doubt each other again.

Finally he broke away. "And you'll marry me?"

"Whenever you want."

There was a patter of footsteps in the hall, and suddenly Amy was at their feet, her arms around both of them as she hugged their knees and looked up.

Laughing, Zack scooped her up into his arms and held her along with Melanie. When Amy lifted her arms to Melanie, Melanie cuddled her close and kissed Amy's cheek with a freedom he hadn't seen in her before.

They were both free to love now, free to create a future together.

Epilogue

It was an end-of-April evening on the island of Kauai. Flo adjusted the white ginger lei around Melanie's neck as Beatrice Martin looked on.

"You look absolutely beautiful, my dear," Bea said as her gaze passed from the wreath of flowers in Melanie's hair down her shimmering, flowing, white silk and chiffon dress to her delicate white shoes. "You'll knock Zack right off his feet when he sees you."

Melanie took a deep breath, anticipating the moment when she'd see Zack for the first time today under the flowered arch the hotel manager had explained would be perfect for their wedding ceremony. This resort was an exclusive one that Zack had chosen specifically for its special services and amenities.

"I still can't believe I'm here," Bea went on. "That man you're marrying is something special."

Melanie knew that. She'd known it from the moment she'd met Zack. The night he'd proposed, he'd insisted he wanted to court her properly. He wanted their wedding night to be the most special night of their lives, and he didn't want to rush anything. So they'd planned the wedding for the week after Easter and had brought everyone with them who was important to them—Ted and Amy, Flo, Bea, Barbara and her husband, John Finney and his wife. Everyone who was important to them except...

Melanie's one regret was that Jordan Wilson couldn't be here to witness the ceremony. His practice kept him too busy for that. Everyone else was here, though.

Over the past few months many things had changed. Ted had become so much a part of their lives that Zack had told him about Melanie's corneal transplants and about everything that had led her to him. Ted hadn't seemed at all buffaloed by it. He'd just patted Melanie's hand and said, "I'm glad you're going to be part of this family." He'd even accepted the gift of this trip to Hawaii from Zack because he knew how important it was to both of them. Flo had been afraid she'd be out of a job, but Zack had insisted she stay on as their housekeeper since Melanie would be working, at least part-time. Melanie, as well as Flo, had become good friends with Bea over the past few months. Zack had insisted the elderly woman accept this trip because he and Melanie might not be together without her and her care of the pink-and-blue baby booties.

"I'm so glad you're here," Melanie responded with a smile at Bea's comment about Zack being a special man. "I'm so glad all of you are here."

There was a knock at the hotel room door.

"That better not be Zack," Flo warned. "All day he's been itching to see you."

Tonight she and Zack would be moving out of the hotel into a small cottage closer to the beach. He'd wanted their nights to be a true honeymoon, even if they spent their days with the people they loved. They'd only be a stone's throw from the suite where Bea and Flo were staying with Amy, as well as Ted who would be keeping the room he'd been sharing with Zack.

Flo hurried to the door, and when she looked through the peephole, she smiled and then opened it.

Jordan Wilson stepped inside.

"Jordan!" Melanie went to meet him.

He took her hands in his. "Zack said to tell you I'm part of your wedding present."

Before their trip she'd given Zack a Vincente Largo sculpture of a man and woman embracing. He'd given her a diamond bracelet she would treasure forever. But apparently he'd also guessed that having Jordan here would make her wedding day complete. "I thought you couldn't get away."

"I wasn't sure I could, but Zack insisted I try. I did want to be here."

If Zack had once been jealous of Jordan, he wasn't anymore. In fact the two men had played golf a few times. Zack had known how important Jordan had been in her life, and she loved her husband-to-be even more for encouraging her friend to come.

"I'm returning to L.A. tomorrow," Jordan explained. "But just seeing you looking this radiant was worth the trip."

"Thank you for coming," she said, squeezing his hands. "It means a lot to me." Then she kissed him on the cheek.

After another hug he winked. "I'll see you again outside."

As Bea and Flo checked Melanie over one last time to make sure they hadn't forgotten anything, her heart began beating faster. She couldn't wait to be Zack's wife. She couldn't wait to be truly one with him. She couldn't wait to be Amy's mother.

The women took the elevator down three floors and walked along a hall with windows facing the ocean. While Bea's cane clacked on the intricately painted ceramic tile floor, Melanie's heart was so full she felt she would burst. Ever since the night Zack had proposed, she'd felt such a sense of peace, such a sense of rightness. She'd had no more dreams, except those of her future with Zack, and no more feelings that weren't her own. All of the puzzle pieces had finally fallen into place, and she knew that Sherry Morgan was at peace, too. It was the kind of knowing that couldn't be explained, only felt.

Stepping outside was truly like stepping into paradise. Palm trees, lush greenery, bougainvillea along with fuchsia and white hibiscus lined the walkway to the private area reserved for weddings. As they approached the arch of flowers, the view of ocean and sky, as well as the kaleidoscope of purple, pink and gold from the setting sun, acted as a backdrop that Melanie would never forget.

The minister stood on the other side of the arch, and then Ted and Zack were there, too. Ted was holding Amy. Though he was Zack's best man, Zack's father wore a flowered shirt he'd bought in the hotel's gift shop after they'd arrived.

Her gaze swept from Ted's wide grin to her husband-to-be. Traditional to the core, Zack had worn a tuxedo. He was devastatingly handsome. The world of love she saw in his eyes drew her to him.

Flo was her matron of honor and walked before her until they arrived at the arch. Then, like Ted, she stepped to the side so only Zack and Melanie stood before the minister. Melanie was aware that Bea and Jordan sat with the two couples on chairs set up for the occasion, but all of her attention was on Zack and what they were about to do. The hotel manager had asked if they'd wanted music, but they'd decided to let the sound of the waves, the rustle of palms and the chirping of birds be their music.

Zack took her hand as they turned to face the minister.

The older man with his white robe, white hair and deep voice began with, ''Dearly beloved...'' Melanie smiled at Zack, and he smiled at her.

Each word the minister uttered went straight to Melanie's heart, and she could see Zack was filled with as much emotion as she was.

When it came time for their vows, Zack faced her, taking both of her hands in his. ''You came to me in a very special way, Melanie. I know we're right for each other. I know you were chosen to be my life partner from this day forward. I know you were chosen to be Amy's mother. Because I know all this, because I feel closer to you than I've ever felt to another person, because I love you with a love that is growing stronger each day, I promise you my life, everything I am, everything I have. I will listen to you and trust you and walk beside you every day of our lives. I vow to be faithful and to cherish you each precious moment we have together. I love you, Melanie, and in the years to come I will try to show you how much.''

Melanie was overcome by everything Zack had said straight from his heart. They'd decided to make their vows this way...to honestly say whatever they were feeling. She was feeling so much she didn't know where to begin.

Then she looked into his eyes and knew anyplace would be the right place to begin. "Not so long ago, I thought I'd lost everything. Then I dreamed of you. My journey brought me to you, to your kindness and tenderness and passion. You and Amy have brought light to my world again, and I can truly see what's important. You are my soul mate, Zack. I can see and feel the love you want to give me, and I want to give you everything I am in return. I promise to love you each day as if it's the only one we have. I promise to stand beside you and honor you and respect you. I will be the best mother I know how to be to Amy. She's already a part of my heart, just as you are. I will try to make our home a haven, a place where honesty and patience and consideration abound. I give you my whole heart today, Zack. I promise you all of my tomorrows."

They were lost in each other.

Although the minister began speaking again, their silent *I love you*s were much louder than any human voice. When Zack slipped her diamond wedding band on her finger and vowed, "I thee wed," his voice was husky. When she slipped the wide gold band onto his finger, her voice trembled.

The minister's blessing fell upon them, gently cloaking them in the knowledge that they belonged together. When the older man proclaimed to Zack, "You may kiss the bride," the last golden light of day lingered on the horizon.

Zack's kiss was the beginning of their future and the assurance of every promise they'd made. Her response was the acceptance of everything he'd offered her, as well as her pledge to love him for a lifetime.

Finally the minister cleared his throat, and Zack gently ended the kiss. Though he leaned away, he kept his arms tightly around her. "I can't wait till tonight," he murmured near her ear.

She whispered back, "Neither can I."

Then everyone was congratulating them. Amy leaned away from Ted toward Melanie and kissed her on the cheek. She took the little girl from her grandfather, and Zack smiled down on them both.

"Let's go celebrate being a family," her husband said.

"I'll second that," Ted agreed, and kissed Melanie on her other cheek, patted Zack on the back and proclaimed loud enough for all to hear, "Everything's right about this, son. Absolutely everything."

As Zack wrapped his arm around Melanie's waist to walk her back to the hotel and their wedding reception, he stopped in the middle of the path and kissed her again. The breeze wafted the chiffon of Melanie's gown around them, and she returned her husband's desire, knowing they were one in spirit, knowing they would soon be one in body, knowing the rest of their lives would be filled with gratitude and love.

* * * * *

*Look for Karen Rose Smith's
next book,*

THE MARRIAGE CLAUSE,

*coming in May 2002
from Silhouette Romance.*

Silhouette Romance introduces tales of enchanted love and things beyond explanation in the new series

Soulmates

Couples destined for each other are brought together by the powerful magic of love....

A precious gift brings

A HUSBAND IN HER EYES

by Karen Rose Smith (on sale March 2002)

Dreams come true in

CASSIE'S COWBOY

by Diane Pershing (on sale April 2002)

A legacy of love arrives

BECAUSE OF THE RING

by Stella Bagwell (on sale May 2002)

Available at your favorite retail outlet.

Silhouette ®

Where love comes alive™

*Silhouette presents an exciting
new continuity series:*

**When a royal family rolls out the red carpet
for love, power and deception, will their
lives change forever?**

The saga begins in April 2002 with:
The Princess Is Pregnant!
by Laurie Paige (SE #1459)

**May: THE PRINCESS AND THE DUKE by Allison Leigh
(SE #1465)**

**June: ROYAL PROTOCOL by Christine Flynn
(SE #1471)**

Be sure to catch all nine Crown and Glory stories: the first three appear in
Silhouette Special Edition, the next three continue in Silhouette Romance
and the saga concludes with three books in Silhouette Desire.

And be sure not to miss more royal stories,
from Silhouette Intimate Moments'

Romancing
the Crown,

running January through December.